A.H. Reid

Moments of Truth

MARY ELLIS

John Murray

For Valerie

© Mary Ellis 1986

First published 1986
by John Murray (Publishers) Ltd
50 Albemarle Street, London W1X 4BD

Typeset by Inforum Ltd, Portsmouth
Printed and bound in Great Britain
by The Bath Press, Avon

British Library CIP Data
Ellis, Mary
Moments of truth.
I. Title
823'.914[F]   PR6055.L49/
ISBN 0-7195-4287-1

Contents

Each to his own

The Hoffmann family lived in one of the less popular New
England villages, in a big house, left over from the
Georgian era, with high pillars on its Greek portico-
porch, a wide lawn, and birch and maple trees, turning to
gold and burgundy-red in the crisp autumn air. It was the
favourite of three households – the other two in New York
and Florida. Adolf Hoffmann was a banker, third genera-
tion German–Jewish, born in Manhattan. He had never
allowed his wealth to change his style of living – his slogan
was 'enough should be enough'; but that somehow did not
arrest his ever-growing fortune. He had married a doctor's
daughter during the Wall Street crash in the twenties.
Rose was a New Yorker and when she and Adolf fell in
love, despite her Christian family's disapproval, they
married and were happy. Adolf became richer and richer,
Rose fatter and fatter. They had three children, two boys
and a girl. The boys behaved as they were meant to, the
girl, Ruth, was a rebel. From the very beginning she
would not grow up as her parents wished her to. With the
two boys safely at college, Rose and Adolf decided to take
Ruth on a long European jaunt for at least a year, hoping it
would broaden her outlook. She had grown into a formid-
able young woman, beautiful, but determined to be her
father's son. She spent every hour he could spare, listening and learning about finance, stocks and shares and
banking, and several hours a week in her father's office.
Her mother was miserable about it, her father jubilant.

7

'Those boys of mine,' he would say, 'they are sissies compared to Ruth! She will be a fine business woman.' Even so, he was a bit worried about Ruth's talent for manipulating people, and the way she made things happen.

It was during their stay in Monte Carlo in the late summer that Ruth met the Honourable James Arrowsmith.

They had eyed each other on the beach. Ruth had her black hair done in a long plait that swung down her bare back – her front wore the minimum of scarlet triangles. She looked delectable – a bright poppy among the ageing houris covered in suntan oil and very little else. As for James, he was a tall, Apollonian young man – awkward and shy. His parents hoped he would be bait for some millionairess – after all it was hard to keep up the estate in Hertfordshire. Of course they did not worry James about this – and they almost never mentioned it to each other.

On the sizzling beach Ruth and James enjoyed a daily intoxicating dose of one another. One morning, after their swim to the raft she said: 'I don't even know your name.'

'Jim – Jim Smith. And yours?'

'Ruth Hoffman.'

'It sounds foreign.'

'I'm American.'

'I know that, by the way you talk.'

'Why are you here? Is it a holiday?'

'I'm here with my parents. I go back to University in a few weeks.'

'I'm here with my parents, too. They are trying to civilise me.'

He took this quite seriously.

'I long to go to America. When you live on a small island with no escape except into the sea, the idea of a vast

8

continent is exciting. I think you're very lucky.'

'But I live in a small town, in a small state in New England. Just as confining as anywhere in Britain. Anyway I love London. It's so personal. I feel one can escape – as you call it – into the minds of people. At home there are no discoveries – people always tell you everything about themselves before you ask for it. Just like I'm doing to you.'

Ruth was flushed and in her usual mood for argument. But James was contemplating her with amusement. It made her say quickly:

'Let's swim back. My parents will be waiting for lunch.'

'Where are you staying?'

'The Hotel de Paris.' And she dived into the sea, reached the beach before him, and hurried away.

James lay on the beach for a while and then dawdled back to the penthouse where his parents spent their Riviera holidays. It was empty when he got there, so he was able to play his guitar. This was forbidden when his father was present – it almost gave Lord Arrowsmith a stroke to see his son and heir, sitting cross-legged on the floor, with 'TRY ME' emblazoned on his T-shirt, strumming and humming. His mother did her best to keep calm – with tears in her eyes. It was sickening, James thought. Today he had an hour to himself before he heard the lift door slam and his father's throaty laughter; by the time the front door opened the luckless guitar was safe in its case, and James strolling on the terrace, looking angelic, as usual.

His father came out onto the terrace, from where, behind pots of geraniums, he could still see the dome of the sugar-iced Casino, and a triangle of blue sea, wedged between the new high-rises. In his mind he still held the vision of an Edwardian landscape, and he suffered the

9

changes with constant irritation. This was focused on his son, who managed to relax under parental disapproval, and cultivate a compassionate sense of humour about his father, and affection for his mother. He knew that his parents had never allowed themselves any freedom in their privileged lives, so bound by convention and protocol. He did not consider that this condition might be in-built in himself. He looked across at his father who was splashing soda into a large whisky. Horace Arrowsmith (an absurd name for him) growled at him:

'I suppose you've done nothing this morning?'

'I swam, and talked to a girl.'

'That, my dear James, is exactly what I mean by nothing.'

'My dear Pa . . .'

'Don't call me Pa. You know I don't like it. Your mother and I drove to Monaco – that, at least doesn't change. This place grows more unbearable every year.'

'Why do you come here then? You always say you can't afford it.'

'Your mother gets frazzled staying in the big house for months. Especially since we have no staff left.'

'There's Ada and the gardener. Seems enough to me.'

'Someday, if you have time in your busy life, I'd like to talk to you seriously.'

'Don't waste sarcasm on me, father. You know I have nothing but time until I go back to Oxford. I want to talk to you, too.'

'No use now – here comes your mother. Where shall we have lunch?'

James remembered Ruth had said 'Hotel de Paris'. He suggested it and his parents looked surprised. His mother said: 'But you hate places like that.' James looked at her. She was sharply pretty. A little faded perhaps, in a flowery way, but her blonde hair was still bright and she had great style. His father was older – getting stout, with a florid face, accented by signs of bad temper.

'I thought I'd conform for once!' James laughed. 'I'll put on a tie. Don't worry – I'll behave myself.' He went indoors, leaving his parents bemused.

'I know what it is,' said his mother. 'He's met someone he wants to see. Or us to see.' Their eyes met, and each knew what the other was thinking. Perhaps money?

'We'll soon find out, Belinda. Anyway the food is excellent in the restaurant.'

'Do I look all right?' Belinda asked.

'You always do,' Horace lied nobly – he'd been doing it for years, skimming over the truth about everything, including occasional lapses of fidelity. He had fallen in love with her when he saw her behind a counter in Boots. Now he was too worried about making ends meet to care about the trivialities of his marital state. On the other hand, Belinda lived only day by day, mismanaging the household and growing more and more distraught. But all this was hidden under the enamel of good manners.

When Ruth reached the hotel, her parents were waiting in the lobby. She dashed past them, saying 'Sorry. I'll be with you in a minute,' and rushed into the lift. A few minutes later she came down again, looking lovely in a crisp cotton dress – her long hair looped in a sleek coil on her neck, which made most of the other female heads, turned to look at her, resemble fuzzy poodles. Her parents preceded her to a table in a corner of the restaurant, already full of very rich people eating very rich food. She enjoyed feeling alien to them, just as much as her parents enjoyed belonging to them. They settled comfortably, the obsequious waiter spreading large damask napkins over their knees, and presenting them with kite-like menus – he stood there, smiling, with the dignity of royalty. Adolf Hoffmann adored the whole charade, and his Jewish face crinkled wtih pleasure.

'Mama, what would you like?'

Rosa looked uncertain. 'Fish, I think, it was so good yesterday.'

Ruth smiled. They were so endearing in their enjoyment.

'Papa – order fish for all of us. And a bottle of white wine. Muscadet.'

At that moment she was struck dumb, for James came in, following his parents – the head-waiter almost bowing to the ground as he led the way to a table across the room, and saying so that everyone could hear, 'This way, milord.' When they were seated, James looked all around the restaurant and waved when he saw Ruth. She smiled and raised three fingers.

'You know that young man?' her father asked.

'I've talked to him on the beach.'

'But he's with Lord Somebody. The waiter said "milord".' Ruth's mother was twittering.

'He told me his name was Jim Smith.'

'Oh. He must be a secretary or something. Nice-looking.' And her father resumed the buttering of bread.

Ruth felt angry. But she enjoyed her lunch and was not surprised when James came over to the table and asked if he might join them for coffee. She felt her father succumb to the charm that shone from James like a beacon. His parents had vanished and Ruth was sure they took their siesta seriously, never surfacing till four o'clock. Adolf was looking hard at James.

'You are on holiday here, too?'

'Yes – with my parents until I go back to University.'

'Your parents?'

'You saw me with them at the table over there.'

'But you told Ruth your name was Jim Smith. That was Lord Somebody.'

James laughed, and explained. Adolf and Rose stared at him so hard that Ruth kicked at her father's foot under the table.

'I can't help it that my father is Lord Arrowsmith. He can't help it either. If I was true to form I'd call myself "the Honourable" – but James or Jim will do for me.' He held out his hand. 'I'm very glad to meet you both.'

So then they ordered more coffee and settled down to the words and music of new and accepted acquaintance. The American–Jewish warmth overflowed and James was caught up in their interest and curiosity. Rose felt sorry for him when he said only nannies had taken care of his childhood. James was having fun telling them about the estate in Hertfordshire and everything they expected to hear about British high-life. But he didn't fool Ruth.

Later Rose and Adolf went up to their room.

'Poor boy,' said Rose.

'What do you mean? He's got everything.'

'No wonder he's fallen for our Ruth.'

'Now Mama, no foolishness. Ruth has her mind on other things.'

'No girl has her mind on other things if someone looks like James.'

'Remember all those boys each summer at home? Let her enjoy herself.'

Adolf took off his jacket. He stretched his arms and opened the door to the balcony. It was a hot afternoon, white and blue and gold; a faint smell of the sea and flowers overcoming fumes of kitchen and petrol. The very silent time of day.

'Anyway, Lord and Lady Somebody won't want anything to do with us – so relax. They have to have pedigreed daughters-in-law, like all good kennel breeders.' Adolf laughed contentedly – he had no chips on his shoulders – but Rose had vague romantic yearnings and did not like to let the matter rest. They were startled by a knock at the door. Rose opened it to a page-boy bearing a sheaf of flowers.

'Pour Madame Hoffmann.' He bowed smartly and pattered away down the hall. Rose closed the door in a daze.

'Maybe they're for Ruth?'

'Nonsense. Read the card.'

'It says "Thank you both for being so kind today. James".'

'So? He's well brought up. Come on now, Rose. It's time we went on our drive, otherwise the roads will start crowding. Where shall we go?'

'Wherever you like.'

Adolf was pulling a sweater over his head, and emerged, hair ruffled, looking like an elderly schoolboy, gleeful and mischievous. He was enjoying Rose's discomfiture.

'Next time you see them,' he grinned, 'remember to curtsey . . . are you ready?'

He came over to where she stood, putting roses and mimosa into the hotel vase, and kissed her cheek heartily.

'They look beautiful.' She put the last rose into the vase.

'So do you. Come on. We'll drive up to the olive groves in the hills.' Rose looked at him adoringly. He held open the door for her, and she gathered up sunglasses, jacket and an over-full handbag, and followed him.

In the pent-house bedroom, all brocade and looped curtains, Horace Arrowsmith closed the shutters. His wife lay

14

on her bed already, in her plain white slip, legs and feet bare. She was very proud of her feet, always smooth, pedicured, with lacquered toe-nails. Their bedroom, wherever they were, was the only place they relaxed. She had learned to play Horace's wife to perfection; in the early days she had had her difficulties – first giving him a son and heir, and then having to manage innumerable servants on the Estate. Even if years had rusted the silver lining she was still naive enough to enjoy having married into the peerage, and she knew Horace's square hard corners hid a heart as soft as an over-ripe plum.

'What did James say their name was?' she asked, pretending to be sleepy.

'Hoffmann. I looked for his name in the hotel register. Adolf Hoffmann.'

'It sounds German.'

'And Jewish. They're from the States. Do you happen to know who Adolf Hoffmann is?'

'No – should I? Is he a crook?'

Horace came and sat on the edge of his bed. He had taken his trousers off, and his hairy legs descended into white socks on shoeless feet. Not a pretty sight, so Belinda closed her eyes and listened to his awesomely lowered voice.

'Only one of the ten richest men in America.'

Belinda shot up to a sitting position, wide awake.

'Good heavens! Do you think James knows?'

'No . . . and it's best we don't say a word. Let him tell us. But I suggest we invite the Hoffmanns and their daughter to have drinks tomorrow. She looks an attractive little thing. James has good taste. Takes after me. Go to sleep now, old girl.'

He threw himself full length onto his bed, and Belinda watched his moustache blow out with slow breaths, on the verge of snores, in less than no time. Then she too, slept. The siesta was on.

Ruth and Jim waited on the beach until four o'clock. They had a plan. It was to get back to where Ruth could listen to Jim's songs and guitar playing, and tell him what she thought of it. They watched from the street-corner till the Arrowsmith Rolls disappeared towards Italy, and then they lifted joyously to the pent-house. Jim was fantastic, Ruth thought; he set the scene, put cushions on the floor, and half-closed the Venetian blinds. Then he brought out his guitar, holding it like a gift, a precious jewel.

'See this? And this curve, and this ivory bit, and how the grain of the wood flows, and the patina like silk –' on and on he went, Ruth admiring, waiting for the music and his voice. She was amazed, when it came, and she sensed discipline and musicianship. It was a full, pleasant sound, his own arrangement of an Andalusian folk-song, adapted to modern idiom; he ended singing the last verse in Spanish with its original haunting melody. When his long fingers winged a chord to finish, he looked at her questioningly.

She said quietly: 'I'm very impressed. No wonder you want to do this more than anything else. Aren't your parents excited about you?'

'Excited? I'm forbidden to play or sing when they're around. They wouldn't know what it's all about, anyway. My mother might – but she has no say in the matter. They're both as unmusical as toads. So behold my hidden self – the rest, Oxford, the estate, is what they expect of me – plus a marriage someday of course.'

'But you're twenty-two years old, Jim! You have to make your own life surely?'

'This isn't America, Ruth. I've got centuries of be-

16

haviour behind me. But I'm on the verge of breaking the rules.'

'Let me help you.'

'How can you?'

'By making you know that it doesn't matter if you give up all that's expected of you. I did.'

'What did you do?'

'Decided to go to commercial college, study banking, defy the usual plan of parties and thinking about men and children and cooking.'

'But you're very feminine.'

'I wouldn't want to be anything else. That's got nothing to do with it, silly. It's a question of breaking through, knowing yourself, and working like mad. Could you? Could you be yourself?'

They were an extraordinary pair; sitting there on the floor, wanting to touch, to kiss, to laugh – but more than that, wanting to work out their destiny, no matter what. They fell silent, feeling fused, one into the other. He broke the spell.'

'I'll get some lemonade. The parents will be back soon. I'll just put this beautiful monster back in its case. Don't move. We must talk. I feel as though the last hour has been the beginning of my life.'

And so it was.

The Hoffmanns were invited for drinks the next evening. It turned out to be champagne, of course. The Arrowsmiths decided that they had nothing in common. It was all pleasant enough, however, until Ruth was asked politely what she 'did'.

'What do you mean?'

'I mean, how do you spend your time – in the States – do they have the same kind of parties for young people? And are you interested in any special charities and sports? Our girls are always so busy before they marry . . .'

Ruth laughed. She might as well throw the bomb now.

'I'm studying commercial law, because I am going to be a banker, like my father.'

She knew how incongruous it must seem to Jim's parents: here she was in a sea-blue chiffon dress, gold sandals on her feet, eyes shining, and their son James saying 'Isn't she marvellous?' The air was thick with disapproval, despite polite leave-taking, with Adolf almost pushing his wife through the terrace door. Ruth lingered a moment and thought she caught a twinkle in Lord Arrowsmith's eye – but his wife's hand in hers felt like cold flannel. James called after her 'See you tomorrow!'

'Well!' Adolf somehow managed to put every possible definition into that one word. Ruth had gone back to the hotel with her parents, and they were sitting in their bedroom as though recovering from shock. Adolf's patience was at an end, he loosened his tie and kicked off his shoes, and looked piercingly at his daughter.

'No, Papa, don't say it. Whatever it is.'

On their terrace Lord Arrowsmith and his wife were on their favourite hobby-horses of anti-American, anti-Jewish, anti-uninherited wealth venom. Jim turned pale.

'I don't care what you think, or what you say.'

'You can't be serious, James,' said his mother. 'She's older than you are, and most unsuitable.'

A few days later Ruth told her father that she wanted to talk to him.

'Well, go ahead,' he said.

'No, Papa – I want a serious business talk. I need your advice.'

Adolf said he would meet her downstairs in the bar at

five o'clock. He was puzzled, but flattered as fathers are when daughters demand undivided attention. Since her twenty-first birthday, there had been a trust for her – she was twenty-five now – but it was understood that any large withdrawals from it would have to be agreed to, by her father; he thought maybe she wanted to buy something very expensive. He smiled as he drank his Bloody Mary in the bar while he waited for her. She was a good girl, so clever and she would never do anything stupid, he was sure. She came into the dark low-ceilinged bar, looking very serious, and said she wouldn't have a drink, because she needed all her wits about her. They sat in a secluded corner.

'Papa. I want to make an investment.'

'So? Have you been reading any recent financial reports?'

'I am serious. I want a hundred thousand dollars from my trust.'

'Gott im Himmel! What for?'

'First, do I get it? It will be paid back within three years. I'll sign a paper to that effect. Say yes and then I will tell you what I plan to do.'

'It's something to do with that young man. Has he asked you for money? I shouldn't wonder. They seem a seedy lot to me. The photographs his parents showed me of their house in England look like a crumbling movie-set. The answer is – NO.'

'Papa, please be serious. Listen to me. I'm going back to New York and Jim is coming with me. I mean to form a company to make him into a great music-man. Believe me, it will happen, and he'll make ten times the money I've asked from the trust. I've never been so sure about anything.'

'You're in love with him.'

'I am not. I believe in him, and intend to make him into a hot business proposition. He doesn't know about my idea. I've heard him play, and sing, and when you do, I swear you'll know I'm right. He hasn't got a chance with that background and mother and father. And he loves Americans and New York.'

'No, and No again.'

'If it was a pickle factory I wanted, you'd say yes.'

'Everybody likes pickles. You're crazy, Ruth.'

'As you sometimes say, Papa, crazy like a fox.'

They argued for an hour. She put the case so clearly that Adolf finally believed her, agreed to her plan, and felt great satisfaction when she glowed with happiness and said he was the best father in the world.

'But don't tell Mama!' they both said this at the same moment, and the bar-tender wondered what underhand business was going on when the elderly man and the beautiful young woman laughed long and loud, and ordered champagne.

Ruth and James behaved like perfect offspring during the next two weeks. Horace felt smugly that they had made their son see reason, and Rose thought Ruth had finished with her summer romancing, when James announced that he was going back to Oxford earlier than planned.

Adolf got their plane tickets, and gave Ruth the keys to the apartment in New York where they were to stay until Ruth found a flat for James. So early one morning, he drove them through the pearly Mediterranean mist to the airport in Nice, where they boarded a plane for New York. As Ruth kissed her father goodbye, he said:

'You make a success of this, or I'll never forgive you. Leave Mama to me. Take care of each other. Keep me posted.' He turned and walked away quickly, and Ruth knew he was crying, as loving Jewish fathers often do.

This is not a fairy-tale.

New York turned a blank face and a deaf ear to James, while Ruth sat at a desk and telephoned every agent, every disc-jokey, every music-factory. After months, she finally struck – if not gold – at least a tinny substance, in the shape of Rob Strong, free-lance, who was working in the record department of a music publisher's. He was a thin, spotty man, with a feverish energy and ambition, plus an unquenchable enthusiasm, and a liking for large bow-ties. He won Ruth's respect, and made James into a popular idol. She had done the spade-work; keeping James to a Spartan routine; no parties, no drinking; practising, composing, voice lessons, guitar lessons, and work-outs at gymnasiums; fighting him, praising him. It suited them both. Ruth shared an office with Rob Strong and a studio flat with James.

When her parents came back to the States she telephoned them every weekend and sent a business letter to her father every month, accounting for every penny, and relating James's progress. James never heard from his father, until the money started rolling in, but he kept up a butterfly correspondence with his mother, the pale blue fluttering airmail paper telling him nothing. His eyes had a burning look when he tore the thin paper to bits. Ruth never asked questions.

The day came when the trust and Ruth's father were paid in full. Music critics had taken James seriously: his talents were 'fresh', 'unusual', 'stimulating' – his songs 'a musicianly hyphen between modern noise and romantic lyricism'. His first two records were successful beyond their wildest hopes; he sent huge cheques to his mother, happy in the knowledge that she could pay off debts, have the roof restored, and tame the garden wilderness. An ungracious acknowledgement arrived each month from her, which plunged him into black moodiness. He had become a cult. Two secretaries were necessary to handle fan-mail and interviews. Rob Strong was on top of the world, Ruth sedately assured, and James unmoved by the nonsense and adulation.

'It won't last,' he said.

One day he asked Rob Strong and Ruth to tell him exactly how much he had in the bank. They named a very large sum, and told him that more would be coming; and all he said was,

'Fine. I have plans.'

Ruth was worried. The charm still worked – but now it was put to conscious use, and she felt he had a secret end in view. Their relationship was still undefined. He put his head on her silken shoulder whenever he was tired; she scrubbed his back in the bath – he bounced into her bed for Sunday breakfast and the newspapers – and once – only once, when he was depressed they had slept in her bed, touching and fitting neatly like two spoons, his back to her, his small rump tucked against her stomach, un-romantic, infant-like – and she had been blissfully content. Ruth began to wonder at this hermaphroditic arrange-ment, and expected him to fall in love any day. She had conditioned herself for this to happen, and knew it would never be with her.

It was a bitterly cold winter. New York is beautiful, crystallised, hushed, on a winter's night. The telephone rang on Christmas Eve, and an impersonal voice told James that his father had died suddenly, and that it was imperative that he come to England immediately. Since he was heir to the title and estate, his presence was deman-ded, not requested. He asked to speak to his mother, but was told she was under sedation. When would he arrive? Ruth only heard him say 'Tomorrow'. And knew this was almost the end of the story.

'No – you are not to come with me' he told Ruth. 'I'll miss you terribly.'

The next morning, Christmas Day, she watched the Concorde rise straight into the air like a dragon-fly. James had gone, stripped bare, even his guitar left in her keeping. His latest record had just been launched, and every time she put on the radio, his voice came over – this disembodied presence gave her no peace. Rob Strong, work accomplished, had gone on holiday, her parents were in Florida. Time to think. If James and she had not met, she told herself, no rebellions would have been fulfilled; he would have gone back, back, back, to his forbears, and nothing would have disturbed the pattern. She knew quite well that it had been her ambition, her manoeuvring that had taken James, and abducted him into an alien world. But not against his will. A seed of guilt began to bother her. What a merry Christmas.

She heard nothing from James for two weeks. And then, at three o'clock one morning, a telephone call. His voice, clouded by three thousand miles, sounded clipped by distress and urgency.

'Can you come over?' he asked. 'I need you. It's important.' Ruth took one minute to think, and two to say she would fly to England the next day.

At the last moment, she took James' guitar in its case, and it took up the seat next to her in the plane, a voiceless companion. A hundred questions rushed through her mind. Iron-grey cloud and piercing cold welcomed her at Heathrow. After an hour at the luggage carousels, she walked through the green exit and found James on the edge of the waiting crowd. She was shocked by his appearance. It was as though his absence had robbed him of all assurance. His eyes, dark shadowed, held no inner light. She kissed him, and he hurried her out to a shabby, muddy car; he held the guitar case carefully, as though it were strange to him, and put it on the torn back seat, with her suitcase, and said 'Thanks'. They were well on the way, when he started talking.

'It was a shambles when I arrived. Not only the garden. The house was hanging on its hinges, peeling, holes in the roof. You'll see. It looks like a Palladian skeleton. I was sick with shock. I still am. Only the old gardener was there – I've known him since I was a child – he taught me to ride my pony; the rooms were icy, uncared for – half the furniture gone, the kitchen a stale mess. Everything horrible, and smelly and neglected. I couldn't believe it. I still don't believe it.' He banged his fist on the steering wheel, and turned to look at Ruth. 'I don't know what to do.'

'And your mother?'

'That's the worst of all.' He stopped the car on the edge of a field. A red winter sun was almost setting. Their breath misted the glass in front of them.

'At the moment all I can get out of her is that the money went to pay my father's gambling debts – his clubs, his liquor, and a mistress she hadn't ever known about. Nothing for her. No servants paid, no bills paid. That dream of setting things straight . . . O God, Ruth – all that work, and what you've done for me – it's madness, but all I can feel is that I should never have left them – never split their lives wide open . . .'

Ruth could not answer him. So they drove on, and after an hour came upon the Arrowsmith Estate, on the edge of a lovely wood, a silver stream cutting through stubbled meadows, and in the distance the sad house calling for help – its shape so beautiful, so wounded, its wide facade divided by a double staircase in broken stone, like a toothy smile – and the high windows beckoning to dark emptiness.

'They even sold the two cars. This one belongs to the gardener.'

Ruth said: 'It will seem better in Spring.' That made James smile and for a second they were as they had been, amused and close – in that second the grief left James eyes and he revved up the shaky car and sped up the long driveway.

In the great hall, a voice cut through the shadows.

'So you've come, Miss Hoffmann.' Lady Arrowsmith rose out of a chair near the big fireplace where a half-blackened log glowed; a very thin spaniel got up and wagged itself towards James. There were no cobwebs, no veils of old lace, but Ruth thought of Miss Havisham and how Dickens had captured vanished splendour and despair and misfortune. She shivered.

'Come to the fire, Miss Hoffmann. The house is very cold. James will make us a pot of tea.'

Ruth sat near Lady Arrowsmith, on a low stool.

'I am so sorry about everything.'

'It's nobody's fault. That money James sent made it possible to start again from scratch. I know I really have you to thank.' She leaned across and patted Ruth's hand, 'I was absurdly prejudiced when we met years ago. My husband always said you would be good for James, and I suppose you were. Forgive me. I'm afraid there's nothing here I can offer you now, except a very historical bed with a damp mattress.' She seemed to think this was very funny. Ruth told her she had a room in the village pub.

'Nonsense. You will stay here, of course.'

James' eyes pleaded with her to agree as he came in with a tray – a brown kitchen tea-pot and three mugs (shades of

25

the Monte Carlo Terrace!) Ruth felt a wild urge to laugh out loud. Even now James' mother could not admit to James' talent and success; for her he must remain the sprig of the family tree, the sole heir and last in line of a decaying dynasty.

Ruth thought, What am I doing here? They drank the black tea by a dying fire, and after it James took her up the wide staircase, and opened the door to a big room. Its narrow casement windows looked down onto an unkempt tangle of thorny hedges through a screen of ivy. Dark blotches of damp shadowed the walls, and here was the high bed, sheetless, pillowless.

'I'm sorry.' James stood, holding her suitcase, staring at her.

'If you get me some sheets, a blanket, and a pillow, I'll be fine. I always travel with a hot-water bottle. It's a terrific bed. I'm sure Queen Elizabeth must have slept here.'

'Only my Aunt Katherine.'

Later, lying awake Ruth decided what had to be done. Her mind was flooded with the vision of her own country; her parents; a realisation of the great benefits given to her — and a deep, abounding pity for James, that must never be allowed to surface. She would stay as long as it would take to arrange for what was now James' fortune to be transferred to his bank in Britain. An accountant and a solicitor would have to be alerted, and James and his mother left in charge.

'Someday I'll come back,' she told herself, 'I'll find everything in order — there will be maids and butlers and gardeners again, and tourists paying to be shown over the house. Maybe there'll even be a zoo. Perhaps James will hold pop music Festivals and the velvet lawns will be packed with long-haired youths and short-haired girls and coke-tins, and James himself playing the guitar.' The moonlight streamed in onto the bed. She lay in a silver blanketed chalice and knew it might never happen. But she must pave the way. It was the right ending to the story. Arrowsmith would be restored to its original beauty, and in a strange way belong to her, too. She wept into her pillow, then.

A rooster trumpeted the frosty dawn; she slid out of the horrendous bed, and remembered her father had promised Florida on her return 'to bake the damp and cold out of you!' She was ready for a big breakfast, and relished James' offering of porridge. In three days the business was done, and on her last evening the gardener's wife cooked dinner for them – some part of a cow with dumplings and carrots. James said the wine cellar was intact, and brought up two bottles, unlabelled and thick with dust. Lady Arrowsmith was in full regalia, black lace and amethysts, endearing and ridiculous in the dreary drawing room. But Ruth felt warm and mellowed, all pain and worry exorcised.

Huddled near the fire an hour later, the conversation lagged. Not for long.

'Of course you and James will be married here, in the old church.' The pause was ominous.

'It's a charming idea, but I am not marrying James. I will be leaving for home tomorrow.'

Ruth looked at James. She was sure she saw relief in his eyes. And amusement. If Lady Arrowsmith had thought it would help matters, she would have fainted.

James drove her to the airport the next morning. On the way he asked: 'Why are you leaving? Is it all so impossible?'

'I've done what I set out to do. I've made you successful and rich. Isn't that enough, my darling? I was right on both counts. We can thank each other.'

Later, as she waited for her plane to be called:

'When we met in Monte Carlo, we were so unknowing – it stopped us in our tracks. The world is getting better, James – but we belong to very different peoples. I shall watch what happens to you. I care for you.'

'I thought you might marry me.'

'I never thought it. We'll both meet our own one day. I must go.'

They stood silent for a moment.

'What are you going to do now?' James asked. Her smile was rueful.

'Invest in a pickle-factory. 'Bye.'

And she was gone.

A Last Fling

The flowering candles were alight on the chestnut trees. A sort of Christmas in Spring, and Iris Arding-Welles withdrew further into the corner of the huge black Daimler that was bringing her back from the solicitor's office. As the car leaped forward at the green light, it jolted her to remembering a flood of things to be done immediately, and turned her eyes inward until she reached home. Home was a de-luxe pent-house, where her factotum Mary, maid and companion for forty years, awaited her with a light lunch on a tray, a dachshund under her arm, and the proper murmur of condolence. That there was an unmistakeable twinkle in Mary's eye, however, and an expectancy in her voice did not escape Mrs Arding-Welles' notice. As she took off her veil and her gloves, even the dark age-freckles on her hands did not depress her any more.

Iris Arding had been one of the lovely ladies of the chorus in the days of escapist musical comedies. Her transparent skin, patrician limbs and natural red hair had made her one of the élite of the show-girls in the golden era just after the First World War. The nonsensical lyrics and tunes had not affected her stance of aloof virginity; usually her one line, spoken in a soft, well-bred voice, drove the younger members of club-dom wild. She bled them dry, without giving herself a wound. Year after year the mixture was the same – the leading ladies disappeared into Limbo, or to the higher ranks of theatre or marriage, but Iris went on; her role inevitably one corny line or a deep curtsey, balancing a paste tiara on her marcelled head before some grease-painted Majesty, who muttered:

'Get up, you bitch, I've got to walk down-stage!'

It went on till she was well over thirty when she met George Percy Welles, son of a millionaire, and just enough younger than she was to fall flat on his fact in abject adoration. There followed a year of the only real acting ever demanded of her; the winning over of his family; the rejection of his wooing, until finally Welles senior begged her to marry his pining son. After all, the Gaiety Girls had married into the best families, and the only modest request was that she must turn her exquisite back on 'The Stage' and its exposures to frivolity. When she accepted this proposition, along with the assurance of money to burn, the dressing room at the theatre, which she shared with six other young women, seethed with excitement. Her last month of performing was a riot of adieus . . . George sent roses every night, and an expensive gift every Saturday; her friends benefited – alas, she had no family to rejoice.

She was frank with the Welles family – there was no trace of her forbears, except a charitable foundling home, and a convent orphanage. Her name should have been Harding, but the little lay-sister whose duty it was to pick the available names for the newly-found infants had dropped her aitches – so Arding it was, and remained. 'Iris' had been her own choice; the nuns had called her 'Poppet', and her play-mates 'Carrots' – but both had seemed unsuitable to the glamour she had in mind; and it was her liking for purple, 'so good with red hair' that determined her floral name.

After the wedding there were years of abundance. A child was born prematurely, to die a little wisp of incubated daughter, and Iris was told by the best in Harley Street that any more children were out of the question. George bore the news well, and they braved it out with the family, insisting that they wished their lives to be childless, and were content for the younger Welles son to provide the heirs.

Iris had made George very happy. He was a good man, and had worked hard and cleverly to amass his millions of pounds. In the third year of their marriage, Iris met some old friends at a first night; with them was a tough American film producer, who had flattered Iris by telling her she looked like Myrna Loy, and should have been in films. She had felt a strange unease, and when she told George about it later he laughed at her across the polished mahogany and crystal of his dinner-table, and reminded Iris that she had never had a scrap of talent. George loved her, and was so sure of her . . . but Iris haunted the film emporia for a while, identifying herself with all the marble-faced women who leaned out from half-an-acre of silver screen. Then she forgot about it in the thrill of new and even better cars, and cruises, and precious stones.

When the Second World War came it coincided with her middle-age. Fortunately she was too busy to indulge in the neuroses and self-pity that so often besets idle women at this time. She bounded over her critical years in WVS uniform, well-nourished on Black Market food supplied by George, whose affairs had become hush-hush and whose office had moved underground. She closed three rooms in their pent-house and 'made do' with Mary and a char; she learned to like rabbit, fish-pie, and dried eggs and lost two stone as a bonus for her good behaviour. Since George had the temperament that inflates itself with worry, no-one realised he wasn't well; and when, after the peace was declared he had a heart attack, it scared them both into realising how many years had gone by, and they began to hoard their health, taking cures abroad and at home until they were both sleek and tidy again after the wracking rumple of war.

In the years that followed, Iris became moody. She treated poor George to a delayed reaction: she spent money on her face and her clothes. She had old photographs enlarged and made a fool of herself in a kind of self-cult, which she knew had no justification. George grew more puzzled, more innocent; he longed for Iris to sag a bit about the jowls and when he said 'getting fleshy, old girl' she didn't speak to him for a week. He couldn't understand her wanting to be the centre of attention and always looked unhappy when his palatial drawing-room was packed with hissing sycophants drinking his gin. Nor did he escape the female boa-constrictors; he unwound their brazen arms from around his neck, and sent them on their hopeful ways.

Nobody was surprised when George died quietly in his sleep, his affairs in order, his will dedicated to his wife 'with thanks for her years of devotion'. Nothing could have been more in tune with his rich and well-bred living than his withdrawn and well-bred dying. He would have been wryly pleased to note that his widow 'didn't make a fuss'.

Indeed not. The Spring day blew softly through the pent-house while Mary served Mrs Arding-Welles with sweetbreads on toast (so light and nourishing) – and stood, awaiting developments.

'We are going away, Mary – I want a change. Italy, I think. Rome, where they make those films. Don't pack much; I shall rent Lady Braden's flat again. We'll leave next week – no car – and arrange to have Suzie put in the kennels. Take the tray – I want to be by myself and think.'

In these orders Mary discerned a heartening resemblance to one Iris Arding of Dressing Room Six, and left the room with a secret smile.

George's family, what was left of it, had been kind. With the proper bequests out of the way, Iris would be a millionairess twice over. She felt exalted, free, and all those things forgivable at seventeen, but unusual at seventy. She had had George, like the long run of a play: enjoyable, but now enough – enough, enough. It worried her a little, wondering what she would do with all the money. There was a house in Paris, a yacht in Cannes, and things she neither wanted nor understood. She would sort it all out when she got back. Later in the afternoon when she telephoned George's office and his solicitor, she sensed their relief at getting rid of her while the estate affairs were settled: they endorsed her visit to Rome: 'Just cable or telephone if you want anything; remember we are here to help you at any time . . .'

I should damn well think so! I don't count now; I'm just the old chamois bag that holds the cash. She suddenly had a vision of a large leather pouch hanging under her Balmain costume as she boarded the plane. 'Has Madame anything to declare?' 'Only three million pounds . . . here!' patting her pelvis. She laughed out loud and rang the bell. Somewhere, somehow, her laughter fell into the laps of the gods.

Rome lay white, pink, yellow, glinting with gold, sharpened with pines. The teasing modernity superimposed on its antiquity was like Hindemith upheld by Bach, and offered almost unbearable stimulation. The bloom of near-evil machinations, thrown like a rose onto the knees of the ready females as they sipped vermouth in the cafés, or leaned against the balustrades of the Spanish Steps, became a pulse-beat in the afternoon sun. Sanity seemed hushed behind the Vatican walls; a fever, not resembling the Henry James Colisseum chill, clinked glasses with Iris, and crept into her veins. The motor horns, the fury and purr of Italian voices grated through the traffic noise; a great smell of sweat, silk shirts, garlic, perfume and petrol . . . a rustle of Pucci shifts, hair-in-the-eyes behind dark lenses, tongue on the lips readiness. Senses – senses – senses . . . More than five, surely . . .?

Sunset on the Via Veneto . . . and, 'You are interested in the films, Signora?' Iris turned; a man who had been looking at her for two days and who accidentally (she wondered), had sat next to her in the cinema that afternoon, had quietly sat himself down at her table. Her first reaction was habitual withdrawal – then she saw he must be young enough to be her grandson . . . almost. She smiled, and in a few minutes they were well away in mutual revelation. He was Filipo Guardi, a film producer. His current inamorata, 'over there, Signora, Rosa . . . she will be a great star, like Sophia.' Rosa saluted across the crowd. Definitely, anything could happen. With the sixth drink, and the shadows purple between the awnings, a meeting was arranged in an office for the following day. Iris got up – she could still hold her alcohol magnificently – and wove her distinguished way between stares, the young man trailing, a new-born smile on his thin lips, a confident sigh swelling his ribs under the pale blue shirt, hips moving beautifully, relentlessly, in too-tight trousers. Men turned to watch the incongruous exit, grinning: 'Ciao, Filipo . . .'

Iris lay in a sun-chair on the terrace of Lady Braden's top floor flat. This was a different Rome than she had known.

Much more violent, much younger. Where the inflamed laziness? Filipo, in an hour had infected her with the urgency of immediate action. For what? She was not fooled. Obviously the woman who kept the porter's lodge in the courtyard could be bribed to tell all she knew – and she and George had stayed here before. A young man would only have to ask, and he would be rewarded with eye-rolling tales of the widow, her past visits, her trunks, her maid, her money-money-money; enough to make his manicured fingers itch – enough to make him plan for the great film that was going to out-do 'La Dolce Vita'. Iris knew, that somewhere at this moment, Filipo was plotting to fleece her – nicely, legitimately.

Mary had gone to church. The dusk was magical; but Iris was suddenly strangely lonely.

By the next morning she had decided to play Filipo's game; with eyes wide open, heart closed, invulnerable – as she had been at that first interview for the Fayre Follies over fifty years ago. It was good to feel she was needed, desperately – even if it wasn't for the red hair, the long legs, the dewy promise. George had taught her the dignity of money. She was no old harridan buying pleasure. She was completing a circle, and cash was wanted.

Twenty-four hours later, she was, verbally, backer and chief share-holder in Cornucopia Films. A rough synopsis of the script was in her hands. She had delayed signing her money away, till she had read it; it was semi-sophisticated drivel, but a plan was forming in her mind. It wasn't much fun being the power behind the throne – if they wanted her money, and they certainly did, Guardi and his Fat Friend would have to give her something for it. She would have her fling. A scene, one scene in the whole big film, written specially for her.

She found Elizabeth Arden's red door – flaming flag of

danger in every capital: age on the way. She emerged refreshed, flattered, massaged, and, from a distance of fifteen feet, a well-ironed fifty.

The second meeting of Cornucopia Films was stormy. But her drooping lids and the emeralds on her fingers were irresistible, and the Fat Friend, whose name was Angelo, inserted the clause in the agreement – a scene must be designed for the Signora to meet with her approval. When the contract was signed, three copies, and the first cheque handed over, Iris left the office, knowing all the conniving that would go on behind her back. Filipo was confident he could cut the inflicted scene after the preview and the wheels started turning. Apart from a flustered cable from George's bank asking why this sum was needed, every-thing proceeded amicably. In London, it was taken for granted that George's widow was slightly unhinged; and the solicitor suggested she might be buying a Mediterra-nean property: very sensible. She was, indeed.

Every day Filipo telephoned, every week there was a meeting and every week Iris watched a day's work at the studios. Innumerable dinners, coffees, arguments. Only one laughable, arm-kissing performance by Angelo, well in his chianti cups. And only one major row; about Rosa's swinging behind, large nipples, and nasal voice. These three things, Iris discovered, were intended to endear Rosa to the world. They were treasured investments. The story was called 'The Birthday' and seemed inexcusable to Iris, but she knew she was out of touch. The twisting hips for instance – nothing new there really – the Charles-ton had been twice as provocative, beads swinging, silken knees parting. She said this to Filipo. His eyes lost their glazed look and burned bright: 'Per Bacco, we've got it,' he yelled.

Her scene would be in a restaurant watching, waiting –

36

talking to the waiter about old times . . . she would wear her most beautiful dress and her jewels, and she would speak in English – yes? It sounded vastly unoriginal, but something made her withhold criticism. Filipo had definitely swallowed the canary. He cleared the studio one morning, except for the cameraman, and one very old actor; and built a corner replica of gold, plush and palms – a Maxims, a Café Royal – unknowingly setting a scene the Signora recognised. When she walked onto the set, it was as if a whole era, violet-scented, fell upon her. She seemed possessed, and it was contagious.

Filipo was at a loss. The script-writer had promised him a dull scene between a rich old lady and a head-waiter – a fill-in until the action shifted to a night-club in the modern idiom where the turgid story could continue. A scene to be cut out and never missed – it had been ordered so. And now this.

They worked for four days, non-stop; Iris insisted on close-ups, changed the lines, and remembered all the old tricks. The scene was well-lit; the bejewelled old lady, aigrettes in her hair, sitting in the corner, had drunk a bottle of champagne. Waiting for a gigolo who never came, she poured out her thoughts to the wine-waiter; her opinions of the world as she saw it, the past as she had lived it – English interspersed with badly-pronounced Italian; café music in the background. When the Charleston struck up behind the palms, she tied up her long skirt with a napkin, and proceeded, within a square foot, to give a perfect performance . . . four cameras coming in on her like cannon. Half-way through it, out of breath, she leaned on the old actor's arm, and looking at him limpidly, asked for a taxi. The horror on the old man's face made her giggle. 'Cut' shouted Filipo's voice – like hot ice.

There was a deadly pause. Iris smelled amazement,

disgust, and admiration – like gun-powder. She pulled her skirt down, and walked off the set.

She remained at Lady Braden's flat until the film was finished. It took three months. Cheque after cheque to Cornucopia Films. Polite hostility; cuff-links to Filipo, ear-rings to Rosa, a lighter to the cameraman. She knew they were waiting for her to go; but before she packed, she got their signatures on a document stating that no cuts would be made in her scene until after the showing at Cannes. She would get over to see it, somehow. Mary had had enough, too. She had seen the Pope once, waving his blessing from a window, and had been pushed and bruised and pinched in a very un-Christian manner in the process. She kept quiet on the subject of Iris' adventure, but had secretly enjoyed every minute of the business. Standing about in the dust and draught of the studio, stumbling over cables, blinded by the lights, holding a mirror and a glass of water – this was just her cup of tea. Long discipline and routine had long since made her forget the delicious freedom of vagabond living; snatched sandwiches and the deep silence and bated breath during performance.

She packed for Iris, lost in tissue paper, trying to get up an enthusiasm about returning to a well-ordered household, a dachshund, and Mrs Sherwood, the cook.

Iris shared her depression. When she boarded the plane, and felt Filipo's kiss on her cheek, she felt she was being forgiven for something. After the first weeks of flattery there had been no real warmth or consideration in the Italian approach. Nothing was sugar-coated these days – bitterness tasted bitter. She embraced the cold shoulder; 'Ciao, Filipo.'

Even ten years ago she would have taken him to herself. She got the sudden feeling that maybe he had expected this. Perhaps she had left something unfinished? The

Opus Eleven

Erika Baumann sat on the terrace, looking towards a flamingo pink sunset. She had just arrived at her villa in Castignières – her luggage was still in the hall. No-one was here to greet her, because it was a day earlier than she had told them – on purpose. She wanted to savour whatever images were left to her after the memorial service in London – where everything that could be said had been said, where the respectful panoply of grief, eulogies for the illustrious dead, the great Austrian composer, 'the unforgettable personality', Eugen Baumann, her husband, had been celebrated. Celebration would have been exactly what he wanted. Now she would have all the time in the world to remember every inch of the way. She would have to go through his belongings. His manuscripts in terrible disorder, (he had never allowed anyone to touch anything in his work-room) all in the big studio built as an annexe to the villa. It had been locked and shuttered for a year.

He had been forty when she met him. World War II was over, and she had just finished school with honours; her father, a London surgeon, Sir Richard Wilmot, was very proud of her and took her to the Baumann concert. She remembered it in detail, her new dress, her father beaming and introducing her to everyone, the thrill of the concert: Baumann playing and conducting one of his own symphonic poems at the end, after the Mahler and Mozart symphonies. The audience had cheered, and she had been swept along with the crowd that filled the artists' room behind the platform. Hero-worship made her mute. This silver-haired man, who looked like a benign bird of prey, his large nose like a beak between piercing eyes contradicting a sensuous weak mouth, smiled at her and greeted her father like an old friend. She did not realise of course that Eugen Baumann thought her a ravishing young creature, and that because her father was rich, well-known and music-minded, he would accept the invitation to be dined and wined and bedded for a week between concert engagements. He brought with him a young man who, he explained, was his right and left hand; he corrected scores, kept the orchestras in order, and saw to the musical commitments. The young man's name was Franz Weiner, and he was pale, with dark circles under his large eyes, and a lock of blond hair that kept falling into them. He was round-shouldered from crouching over music-stands, and when he was tired, he rubbed his eyes with his fists like a sleepy child. Then Eugen would slap him on the back and laugh, and say: 'Wake up, you oaf, I need you.' And everyone would think how genial and kind Eugen was. 'O God' sighed Erika, 'I thought so, too.' She had been enchanted by the great man and flattered by his attention. When he left his father's house to return to Vienna, he held her hand for a long time, gazed into her eyes (he knew just how long a look it should be) and said:

'We will meet again very soon; It has to be.' He had put his hand under her chin, his long beautiful fingers slightly caressing, and deposited a tight-lipped kiss on her forehead. It had all worked before. She felt struck by lightening. Franz stood by, the lock of hair falling into his eyes, a suitcase in each hand. He just nodded to Erika and went outside to put the cases into the waiting Rolls-Royce. As Erika remembered it now, it was a ludicrously theatrical scene: but then, she was overwhelmed, in love as only eighteen can be in love; she lost her appetite and wandered around in a dream, as the days darkened into winter. She asked endless questions about Eugen Baumann; she looked him up in the encyclopaedia, and found out that he had been born in Vienna, in the ghetto, and had been taken by his refuge-seeking parents to the ghetto in New York (all ghettos everywhere are the same), when he was an infant. There he had been subsidised by an American millionaire, when his talent was discovered. Everything was grist to her romance-grinding mill. Her kind father (alas, her mother, bored by kindness, had run off long since with a captain in the Army) wanted Erika to be happy, so he suggested a trip to Vienna in the Spring, engaged rooms at 'Sacher's', and wrote to Baumann, who was to be conducting concerts there. He received an enthusiastic reply, assuring him of a great welcome and seats for every performance.

So on an April day, when myriad crocuses were carpeting the parks, and the optimistic young were shedding outer garments and lifting their faces to the sun, Erika and her father arrived in Vienna and Sacher's Hotel. The rooms there are still haunted by shadows of Arch-Dukes; the alcoves, chaise-longues, crystal chandeliers, heavy paintings, enhanced by a wealth of gold-leaf, and every shade of faded red damask, breathe the lost fragrance of waltzy amours. And of course the vague smell of chocolate, coming from the kitchen, where the world-famous Sacher cakes get baked by the dozen every day.

Erika's room overlooked the opera-house – just across the square, and Eugen Baumann had sent three dozen roses, deep red, to await her arrival. There was a lot in the newspapers about him. It seems he made a point of including one of his own works at each concert, and the critics seized upon them. They had no titles – only 'opus' numbers – he had reached number ten, and the critics voted it cold, cacophonic, lacking in melody, but majestic and compelling. In an interview, Baumann said that when he had composed a dozen symphonies, he would retire. And when would that be? 'In about twenty years.' And so on, and so on. His professional smile would flash, final as the slamming of a door.

Erika's father was distressed. He had not bargained for the ardent wooing of his young daughter. He could find no valid excuse to turn the great Maestro down as a son-in-law. His reasoning and mistrust were swept aside, and Sir Richard, aware of his daughter's love for the man, finally agreed to the marriage.

It was all too easy. Erika and her father were invited to Eugen's chalet in the Salzkammergut for a weekend, and there, one night, Erika was deflowered, and sadly disillusioned about the fusion of ardent bodies. Eugen behaved as though nothing had happened – and indeed, in his reasoning, nothing had; he had asked Sir Richard for the hand of his daughter, and had been accepted. She was therefore already his. Of course Erika did not tell her father. She suspected that even in the nineteen-forties, there would have been an old-fashioned duel with pistols.

So, she and her father returned to London, to order a trousseau, and arrange for the wedding. Eugen wrote to her every week, and sent extravagant gifts. A ring with a pigeon-blood ruby weighed heavy on her hand. She had to take it off to practise the piano every day. She considered this her duty now – in view of her future. She lived in a dream, trying to forget the loss of her virginity in what her father called 'Yodel-land'.

They were married in the late summer, in time for Erika to accompany Eugen on a continental tour, before they settled into his flat in a fashionable London square; where two outsize concert-grand pianos took up a platform in the living room; and the whole place was geared and furnished for bachelordom. She managed to squeeze a dressing-table into the marbled bathroom, and used a former guest-room for her personal belongings. Eugen was not interested in these changes – so long as she was sure to be in his large bed waiting for him, at any time, any hour.

The tour had been a disastrous honeymoon. Because of his work (he was, he said, in the throes of composing Opus 11) they had separate bedrooms. He rested a lot, waited on by Franz, who seemed to be secretary, music-counsellor and nurse-maid. When Erika asked if she could help in some way, Eugen would say:

'No-no-no. You are my wife, my queen.'

She, who wanted above all things to be his friend, felt cheated. Sometimes he called to her to come to him as dawn was breaking, and he would take her to himself in a mannerly, impersonal ecstasy, and send her back to her room. She would weep a little then, but at nine o'clock that same morning, quite cool and in command of herself, pour his coffee and smile at him across the breakfast-table in the salon of the hotel-suite wherever they happened to be. Franz would come in, and never raise his eyes to look at her, but sit down and discuss the work and rehearsals of the day, and any musical problems that had arisen; that lock of blond hair over his eyes was in a perpetual state of vibration. Sometimes there would be pages of music manuscript to correct. Erika noticed that Eugen hardly looked at them. After an elaborate almost feminine per-formance of showering, shaving, and the choosing of a shirt, he would vanish until it was time to rest again, and perhaps eat a poached egg, and have a glass of champagne before the concert. It was Franz who told her to come to rehearsals, where he would sit beside her and explain all the misbehaviour of woodwind, double-bass and clarinet, and they would listen and watch, while Eugen stopped their playing with fury, or sarcasm, or childish jokes, according to his mood. He would shout, and wave his arms about, streaming with perspiration, and break a few batons in half. She often wanted to crawl under the seat with shame at these outbursts, and was surprised that the musicians didn't down instruments and walk out.

'They all know he is right, and they love him,' was how Franz explained it, his eyes sparkling. When the tour was over, she felt that she knew Franz better than her husband. It was Franz who told her she was beautiful, it was Franz whose soft voice begged her to be patient with the Maestro who was so precious to them both; and it was Franz who played her bits of the new symphony, which he assured her, she had inspired. Nothing had been as she imagined it, but she was determined to make a success of being Eugen Baumann's wife. And it had seemed to the whole world that it had been so, for over twenty years. Everything had been correct, her intelligent dealing with public life, her appearance, her modest behaviour in the shadow of her husband, the perfect hostess in their three much-photographed houses. This one, where she was now, her favourite, Castignières, facing the Mediterranean on one side, the olive groves and hills on the other. Her father, over seventy, was coming to stay with her. She looked forward to that return to her childhood. But now she must try to remember the years of devotion and pride that had made it possible for her to find excuses for their emptiness. 'Opus 11' had been acclaimed as Baumann's most beautiful composition – 'for the first time, deep emotional tonality, sweeping to a climax'. She had found nothing in Eugen's nature to match it.

There had been one delirious summer. It had been when Eugen was having a cure at Aix-les-Bains, where he held his painful hands under healing hot vapours, and wallowed in mud-baths. She had walked with Franz in the meadows and woods. One day, a stream of words poured out of him, the adoration and frustration of years, and his bleak unhappiness. They had sat under a pine tree, her arms around him, rocking him, his head on her breast. And she had finally been able to push that lock of hair out of his eyes; this belonged to the way of love she had longed for. The fulfilment they found had made her more able to continue the barren splendour as Eugen's wife. They both knew such joy in each other had to end. And then, during the next few years, it was ended for them. Franz fell ill – those shadows in his face had been the banners of disease. Erika's father had understood her anguish and had been helpful – as he had been all through the years – but even the best doctors could do nothing for Franz. He died in a sanatorium, no-one near to mourn him. Erika and Eugen had been a continent away, here in Castignières. When they got a telegram one morning, he had said to her:

'You will miss him a lot, I am sure. In every way. So shall I.' And he had walked away. So he knew.

He had been away for hours, and when Erika found him, late in the day, he was lying on the sand, the little tide-less waves touching his feet. She had sat down beside him, and he looked at her as if he had come back from some far-away place, all the fire and excitement that he had lived by, gone from his eyes; and as they walked back to the villa, he held on to her like a tired old man.

Erika turned more and more to the business of her husband's career. He was almost impossible to live with. He sent away one assistant after another, and she softened their dismissals with encouragement and cash. Eugen's temper flared, and he would yell at the orchestra in rehearsal, and they grew less co-operative. Then the critics started to nag him. They were waiting for another new work from him, like greedy ogres, and they suggested that he had lost his touch and should retire. Was 'Opus 11' his last contribution? Erika suffered for him. Sometimes, in the morning she would find his study littered with manuscript music – all in his spidery writing – note upon note blotted, a night's work crumpled or torn to shreds, spread out on the desk or on the floor. Once, what seemed the beginning of a letter, addressed to no-one: 'I cannot – it is useless.' Struggles of solitary, tragic defeat. She did not dare talk to him about it.

Then she had an idea. A series of concerts to be arranged, all of his eleven symphonies to be played, spread over four performances. In Vienna first, of course, and if it caught the imagination of the public, Paris and London, to follow. Eugen was happy, and for a month it was like old times – his enthusiasm and lust for work returned. The memory of Franz was like an open wound for both of them, a bond of pain. And so, they were closer than they had ever been.

It was during the last two concerts in London that Eugen felt unwell. The Albert Hall was cold, and he caught a chill. He struggled through the final concert, hardly able to stand up to acknowledge the applause; Erika had bundled him into the car, and nursed him through the night. The next day he was rushed off to hospital. And the day after that Eugen Baumann was dead. A nightmare week began; the press, the funeral, the memorial service, and people, people, people, asking questions that Erika could not answer. She was requested by the solicitors to go through all his papers as soon as possible – that is why she was at Castignières, facing a

Mediterranean sunset – all Eugen's real work had been done here, at the villa. She would start to look through everything tomorrow, she told herself.

The next morning Lucie, the cook, arrived early, bringing a bouquet and suitably dressed in dusty black; she was shocked at the sight of Madame – she expected deep mourning and a black-edged handkerchief, and here was Madame in a yellow pyjama suit, ordering her about as though nothing had happened. She was given a long list of things to be bought at the market, and told to get the guest room ready (the one with the balcony and a view of the sea) because Madame's father would be arriving. That, at least, seemed right and proper to Lucie, who had to be satisfied, and go about her business. After all, Madame had given her the triple kiss, and thanked her for her sympathy. The English were peculiar.

Erika opened the shutters in Eugen's work-room. Sunshine flooded in, its rays almost solid gold, thick with dust and motes. She opened the windows, and sprays of purple bougainvillea sprang at her; the door to the terrace would hardly move – so warped by the heat and mistral winds. The piano, tightly shut, waited for its keys to be touched, to give it the kiss of life. The big working desk was covered with letters, papers, newspaper clippings – and here, a metronome: Erika undid the catch and its clock-like pulse, the musician's heart-beat, made the room come alive. Everything seemed busy, insects flew in at the window, and a swallow flew by, disturbed from its nest under the roof-tiles. Her own portrait looked down at her from the white-washed wall. It had been Eugen's favourite – Erika at the time of her marraige, her black hair drawn tightly into a scarlet ribbon, watchful grey eyes in a pale, childish face. She was tempted to take it off its hook and hide it. As she piled papers into boxes, to be carefully looked over,

49

she found old programmes, fan-letters, photographs, newspapers – all to be burnt and forgotten. The solicitors had talked about copyrights, of music-scores – she opened the drawers in the desk and only found a ruler, a magnifying glass, pens, and several packages of manuscript paper, already stamped with expectant musical staff-lines. One drawer was locked, and it was then that she remembered the key she had found in the velvet box with Eugen's pearl studs and two gold watches, and the emerald cuff-links. She had wondered what it would open.

She drank a glass of wine on the terrace, slowly. The blue parasol was open, above her, the silence weighed heavy. There was no hurry now.

In the evening she went back to the work-room. The key from the velvet jewelcase opened the drawer easily – it was wide and deep; lying in it neatly were two bundles of letters tied with string and several large flat packages marked 'original scores'. It was like coming upon Aladdin's Cave. Erika recognised her own letters to Eugen. She knew the writing on the other bundle only too well; that round, even lettering, so easy to read. On the first folded page, so that she could not fail to see it: 'My beloved Eugen' and at the end, 'Your own Franz'.

Her hands shaking she reached for the flat packages still lying at the bottom of the drawer – inside were the hand-written scores – eleven of them – clear notes in assured array – each symphony recognisable from the first bar, marked with the musical punctuation so familiar to her: Each one unmistakably in that same round hand, dedicated to Eugen Baumann. Only on Opus 11 a slight difference – it was dedicated to her.

Aunt Lucy

It was really all Chrissie's fault, Miss Lucy Denton, spinster, kept reassuring herself that this was the cause of the predicament. If Chrissie had come to spend Christmas, it never would have happened. And now she was scared. She let herself into her little house on Blackberry Hill, not even noticing the early crocuses starring in her front garden. The house was chilly, as it always was when she came home from her day's work at the post-office. She took off her sad little blue felt hat, and her slightly damp coat; her coat never seemed to get quite dry all through the winter; and stared at herself in the hall mirror. The one bulb hanging in its shade from the ceiling didn't help her tired face. She saw high cheekbones, kind eyes and a large mouth – all very familiar, brushed over with the grey shadows of middle age and weariness.

If only she hadn't done that ridiculous thing! She remembered how lonely she had been on Christmas Eve, when the whole of the holiday stretched before her without gaiety or company – because her niece, Chrissie, had sent a telegram saying she 'couldn't make it' this year – and 'so sorry' and 'have a merry Christmas'. So Lucy had sat down with her disappointment to read the newspapers; and there, in the column, had been the notice from Thomas Adam, from an address in Germany.

'Lonely school-teacher desires to correspond with equally lonely lady back home.'

That was all it said. And on that fateful night Lucy

Denton wrote her first letter to a stranger.

After three months letters were speeding like frantic pigeons to and from Munich to the small village near the Downs, halfway to the sea – and Lucy Denton was unaware of life around her. She had never written lies to Mr Adam: she had merely avoided any definite truths, and the letters were outpourings of her well-stocked mind and adventurous spirit. For Lucy had had her hopeful days. When she was a young student once upon a time she had loved one Richard Hull very much and, when he had decided to marry her sister Alice instead, she had behaved perfectly. When he had gone away, leaving her sister and children, Lucy had still behaved perfectly, and had taken the whole miserable little family to live with her. If it hadn't been for the house on Blackberry Hill, this couldn't have happened. But Lucy's father had left it to her, lock, stock and barrel, and very grateful she was, too. The years passed pleasantly enough, the children grew up, and until Lucy's sister became ill, their lives were serene. But then despair crept slyly into every corner; and after three years it almost came as a relief when Alice died in her sleep, leaving the two boys and Chrissie to Lucy.

At that time, there was no room for hope in Lucy's heart; life was too difficult to think of anything. The boys soon left Blackberry Hill; but Chrissie stayed. She stayed, beautiful, discontented, but a perpetual challenge to Lucy.

Then finally, one evening, she packed her bags and left. She had won a beauty competition, she said, and she was going to be a model in London. Lucy stared with astonished eyes – and Chrissie threw down a photograph of herself, rather angrily. 'That's the picture that won it for me; you'd better keep it!' And that was that. Chrissie had come back to Blackberry Hill for two Christmasses with chocolates and unusable gifts. She sent occasional letters, which Lucy answered immediately; Chrissie's letters echoed her nature: secretive, and extremely ungrateful. Lucy didn't mind; she had long ago had her emotions nipped and chipped and frosted over. It would have surprised her to receive consideration or tenderness from anyone.

When Chrissie left, Lucy had taken on a job at the Post-Office. It was a small post-office, with nothing much to do – but Lucy knew everyone in the village and knew every letter, and correspondent in the incoming and outgoing post. So her days were full, her sympathies occupied, her heart a closed book. It was a vicarious living-of-a-life for her.

Then came the third Christmas, and Thomas Adam, and the start of those letters. At a so safe distance.

It was March when Lucy got a letter (the fiftieth), asking for her photograph. When she read it, she was eating her supper and she laid down her knife and fork; the scrambled eggs went cold, the tea brewed itself to a black syrup. Her knees shook as she got up from the table and started walking from corner to corner of the kitchen.

'Oh No, oh no,' she cried, 'Besides, I haven't got one.'

At that moment, the great deception was born. And two hours later she sealed a letter to Mr Thomas Adam enclosing the photograph that Chrissie had left with her: the photograph that had won Chrissie the beauty prize and the job as a fashion-model. The empty, chiselled face of a selfish young woman, so belying the warm words written in Lucy's best Madame de Sévigné manner. Her heart missed a beat as she stamped this great lie and sent it across the North Sea to Germany.

June came, a blaze of sunshine and summer glory. The house on Blackberry Hill thrived in summer. Its fresh, white muslin curtains billowed in the warm breeze: it rested, a smiling, almost animate thing, on its little hillock, a quiet content spreading into its garden so humming with bees in and out of flowers in full bloom.

Lucy was having her month's holiday – her greying hair bound up in a pirate's red-spotted handkerchief, her slenderness brown and supple, bending over flower-beds.

Thomas Adam had not written for over a month. Lucy was relieved, because since he had received Chrissie's photograph the tone of his letters had changed. Imperceptibly at first – undoubtedly later. They became shy and serious and uncommunicative: this hurt Lucy at first, but then she laughed quietly at her own folly, and thanked heaven that she had been let off so easily. It was balm to her conscience to think she had made someone happy by that deception. She pictured Mr Adam, thrilled with Chrissie's picture and her own strangely unmatching letters, his loneliness alleviated, his spirits lifted. What she did not know was that Thomas Adam was speeding homewards, to settle his mind. He was suffering acutely from a titilating paradox – a seemingly romantic literary correspondence illustrated by a minor Marilyn Monroe. He could not put one and one together. So he was on his way to Blackberry Hill, to have it out with this phenomenon.

He arrived just as Lucy, hot and exhausted, with garden soil smudged on her nose, was going indoors to fix her lunch. She was hungry, and so rather annoyed when a tall, oldish man stopped at her gate. He was, she noticed, looking cool and expensive. He wore no hat and was most polite. From her doorway, she couldn't see him, but his voice carried comfortably across the little garden.

'I am looking for Miss Denton.'

'Yes?' Lucy was grateful later that the monosyllable had meant nothing really, because the next moment she clung like an agonised vine to the door.

'Will you say that Thomas Adam would like to see her?'

In the minute that seemed an eternity, Lucy's brain worked fast and furiously and it is to her credit that she managed to tell only the truth. There would have been far too much explaining to do later if she hadn't.

'I'm afraid she – she is not here – but I am her aunt. Won't you please come in?'

Lucy will never know how she moved through the next few minutes. She ushered Mr Adam into the little room where she had written all those letters to him; she gave him a cigarette, a glass of sherry, and finally excused herself – 'to wash some of the garden off me. I'll be back in a moment.' Thomas Adam said it was quite all right, and not to hurry. So Lucy found herself, her pulses pounding and feeling very sick, in the safety of her own room.

She didn't try to hide anything from herself:

'This is my penance, for the nonsense' – and so she put on her plainest cotton dress, didn't powder her nose, and brushed her grey hair behind her ears. But she couldn't stop it curling on her neck as though she were sixteen instead of sixty.

'You know,' said Mr Adam, leaning across the kitchen table, 'I'm going to tell you something. I'm very relieved that Lucy isn't here. But I felt I *must* see her – her letters have been so wonderful, and have got me over an awful crisis. Did she tell you about me?' Mr Adam looked as though he had to know. So Lucy said that she had even been allowed to read some of his letters.

'Really?' He looked worried. 'And then she sent me that photograph . . . and that sort of finished it. You see . . . it scared me. I'm a simple man: I had no time while I was teaching to experience or acknowledge certain things, and beauty like that worries me – and she is so much younger than I expected; I thought from those letters Lucy was

55

quite different – more homey and homely, if you get me – and for a time, I suppose, I hoped I'd found someone I'd been looking for . . . the letters were so full of humour – rather old-fashioned and gentle. I can't say exactly what I mean . . .' So the words had come pouring out of him.

Lucy nodded gravely. 'She *is* very beautiful, my niece. I'm afraid when you didn't write to her for over a month – well – she's very young. She's gone to London, you know. She has lots of friends there . . . she's working as a model.'

There was a long pause. Thomas Adam was looking hard at Lucy. He said: 'I'm glad I didn't have to disappoint her. I'm too old for such a young, clever, beautiful girl. I could never risk going on with it. I'm sure you understand.'

Lucy agreed silently, nodding with perfect aunt-shaped dignity.

'It's so odd,' said Mr Adam. 'From those letters I would have imagined Lucy to be more like you, Miss Denton.'

'Elderly and homely?'

'*Just* so! And very easy to be with. By the way, what is your name?'

'Lucy. My niece was named after me. But she likes to be called Chrissie – Christine, on account of her job, you know.'

A twinkle in his eyes seemed to spill over into his smile. Lucy felt the blood rush to her head.

'Would you like some coffee, Mr Adam?'

'Thank you.'

Lucy rushed into her kitchen. Her hand was shaking so much that the instant coffee showered down like bronze snowflakes as she spooned it into her best cups. She was sure Mr Adam enjoyed rich Expresso coffee whenever he wished. She was glad the milkman had left cream that morning.

56

Mr Adam seemed quite happy with his coffee and they were soon talking like old friends – which indeed they were. Lucy liked his deeply lined face, his coarse close-cut grey hair – in fact everything about him. She gave no thought to herself – so lacking in coquetry, she was nearly irresistible, but Mr Adam resisted. Lucy finally said:

'I have something I must tell you.'

'And I already know what you are going to say: the letters.'

'Can you forgive me.'

He leaned across the table and took her hand.

'Listen to me carefully; those letters of yours were the most splendid thing that ever happened to me.' He paused, seeming to make a decision, and said:

'My wife had left me, after twenty years – she went off with a young man who was my pupil. I felt ashamed and doubly betrayed – do you understand? You gave me back some self-respect, and an excitement about living. Wasn't that worth your compassionate little lie? I think so. And I will never forget it; I am so grateful for it.'

Lucy wasn't exactly in shock, but she was unable to collect her thoughts. She had not been nearer to human misery for years, than a village tooth-ache, childbirth or bereavement. And now that her brain, her nerves, her heart were flooded with a hot wave of feeling, she could hardly bear it. Mr Adam seemed unaware of her confusion, and went on talking comfortably:

'I've brought the photograph back to you. I'm afraid it's a bit crushed from being in my wallet.' He put it down on the table. Lucy did not want to look at it or touch it. She would put it back in its frame later, she thought.

'Will you stay to lunch?' she managed to ask in a thin small voice.

'I wish I could. But I must catch the train back to

London. I have to be in Munich again tomorrow. I borrowed this day from the school, saying it was a matter of great urgency.'

He smiled, and his smile hurt her most of all.

'Of course; you could have written. I would have understood.'

'Would you? Anyway I wanted to see you.'

He stood up, so much taller than Lucy, and she felt the world slipping away from her.

'You will still write to me? I can now imagine you as you are, when I get the letter.'

Oh yes, Lucy thought. 'Homely.

'Perhaps.' She said this so sharply, that he looked at her as though he was seeing her again for the first time.

'It's been wonderful; and thank you.' He made the gesture she expected – he kissed her hand. Her rough, reddened, kitchen and gardener's hand.

'Thank you for coming to see me.'

She waved as he closed her garden gate and started almost running to catch his train. Later that day she put Chrissie's photograph back into its silver frame, and sat down to do some mending. The telephone rang. It was Chrissie. Her voice was strident.

'Hello Auntie,' she shouted – 'I'm off to the South of France to do some fashion stuff. So I won't be able to see you this summer. Sorry. Are you all right? Anything happen?'

'I'm fine. Nothing's happened. Enjoy yourself.'

She went into the garden. The sun was going down, and the pale roses had turned flamingo pink in its setting rays. A blackbird was calling insistently.

Lucy took in a deep breath of the summer evening, and turned back into her cottage. There, she put on the lamp on her desk, sat down, and started to write a letter.

Legend

His name was Alexander, and we met in Greece, one evening on the terrace of a café, in a haze of candlelight, yellow roses, wine, and couples dancing against the view of crumbling pillars under a lime-green sky. I had noticed him for days, taking photographs, obviously wanting to be left alone, so I kept my distance, knowing he would talk to me when and if he wanted to. On this particular evening, the terrace was crowded, and I tilted the chair opposite me, reserving it for him, just in case. And he came, looking wonderfully Olympian, tall, his face sun-tanned and cruelly lined, a head of short grey hair, and wearing a fisherman's smock of faded red cotton, the camera on a brown strap hanging across his chest. When he asked if he could sit with me, his voice was bronze. Nothing I write can describe him. I felt the Greek landscape belonged to him, and he made me believe in legends.

It was the beginning of a long friendship, and I know he will not mind if I tell his story.

His father had married a beautiful Greek girl, Elena, after the war, and brought her back to London. When their children were born, they moved south to a lovely rambling house a few miles from the sea. Alexander adored his sister, Olivia, two years younger than he was. They were inseparable, they knew every tree, every flower, every weed in the big garden; there were white fan-tail pigeons, and white ducks on the pond. Alexander had a white goat, and such a great intimacy with the gentle creature, that he was propelled into the bath-tub when he came indoors, and scrubbed with ivory-soap to get rid of the smell. Beyond the pasture fence there was a bluebell wood, where they would play on hot afternoons – or sometimes fall asleep in the sweet-smelling hay-loft, where the pigeons strutted and gurgled. In the late summer they carried pails almost as big as themselves, to pick the blackberries along the hedgerows. A governess came in the mornings, because the school was too far away – and they were taught together, even though Olivia was really too young. The governess was Miss Selby, and later, when they went to school, she stayed in the household. Their parents were away a lot, cruising, motoring, taking sulphuric waters in foreign spas, visiting grandparents in Greece. Almost like strangers when they came home.

Up to the time that Alexander was seven (and Olivia five) they slept in the same room, were bathed in the same high tub, liked the same puddings, and if Alexander was punished, Olivia insisted on being punished too, even if it hurt – she would not have him experience anything without her. As she grew up, she realised he was more beautiful (everybody said: 'What a lovely boy – what a shame his sister doesn't look like him.') And she contemplated her little face in the mirror ruefully. She had a shock when he closed the door between their bedrooms, and wrapped a towel around his loins when she surprised him one morning. These things were wounding.

'Don't barge in like that' he had said crossly, and she slid out of his room feeling like a flower mowed down. (She always insisted she could hear the dandelions scream under the lawn-mower.)

Alexander was twelve when he was sent away to school and he was quite unprepared for discipline and separation.

Olivia had Miss Selby to contend with alone. And the family's priest, Father Anselm. He had been there since she could remember, presiding in the small Catholic church in the village. That was one of the reasons the big house had been bought. Elena belonged to the Orthodox Greek church, and she insisted on religion remaining an important part of her life, and felt that her children should benefit also. Alexander said his prayers at night, and that was that. Olivia grew introspective about it all, and Father Anselm saw his chance, when she was left alone for weeks on end with Miss Selby. He came every other day at tea-time, and spent an hour or so, to Olivia's delight – as poor Miss Selby was sadly lacking in imagination and a sense of fun, and the priest was over-laden with both. He kept laughter surfacing; his Dutch ancestry supplying a Breughel-like simplicity. When the parents came home every two months or so, he withdrew discreetly to his duties in the church. By this time, Miss Selby officiated as housekeeper, and Olivia found it difficult to relate to her parents, even though she knew that they loved her. But when Alexander came home for school holidays he and Olivia were the sun and moon of their own special world, an unspoken closeness, his tempered by caution, hers fearless, overspilling with love, a passionate dedication, even at fourteen. The real sufferer was Father Anselm, who trusted she would grow out of such emotional turmoil. Outsiders would say 'How wonderful to see a sister and brother so fond of one another', as they cycled by. And Olivia grew in beauty and became the eternal Eve.

At eighteen Alexander went to Cambridge, and Olivia was sent to boarding-school. Alexander, freed of all responsibilities except his study of archaeology, flourished and glowed in the new environment, and his vanity was nourished just enough to make him self-assured. His

61

rooms were comfortable, and in the evenings filled with friends sharing in uninhibited argument, laughter, strong wine – sometimes music, sometimes young women, long-haired and studious (in the day-time), seeking pleasure in his company, which they got, in full measure. A photograph of Olivia in a silver frame watched it all in imprisoned cardboard arrest, unless Alexander remembered to put it face-down until morning. The feel of her was with him constantly, disturbing; a girl's face on the pillow would suddenly become hers, and so ended several would-be adventures. He talked about it to Anton, his Austrian friend, who laughed and said it sometimes was worse, if it was a mother's face that ended things.

'Dr Freud has explained all this long ago. I will give you some books.'

He found Anton looking at the photograph of Olivia quite often, and promised to take him home at Christmas to meet her and his family. (Anton looked rather like Franz Schubert, and studied law – 'England has the best legal system' he said, 'but I prefer music.')

Olivia was resigned. She endured school, rather than used it. She did not like the girls; she thought them devious and deceitful. Most of them looked forward to marriage, a few had careers in mind, and all of them were forced to devote hours to languages and physical training. When asked by the head-mistress what she wanted to prepare herself for, she murmured, 'Life'. The poor lady sitting behind her desk in a lavender tweed suit, adjusted her bi-focals and sighed.

'My dear Olivia, we all have to accept that, whatever it brings. You would find it helpful to have a goal of some sort.'

Olivia tried to explain that she was waiting to get some hint from life itself, as to what she should do about it. It wasn't as though she had any special talent. And she was only seventeen.

Christmas that year was supposed to have been fun; full of holly and mistletoe, presents, a huge Christmas tree – everybody at home, and Alexander there with his best friend, Anton. There were lots of parties, and the parents were welcoming, but Olivia felt they would rather have been somewhere else. Miss Selby held the household together, and the festivities seemed a little forced.

One night there had been a big dinner, and Olivia was listening enthralled to Anton's descriptions of Vienna. When the guests had all gone they wandered into the hall where, under the crystal chandelier, a great bunch of mistletoe swung gently, its waxy berries gleaming, a bright red ribbon trailing. Anton, rosy and determined, held Olivia by the shoulders, pulled her under it, and planted a purposeful kiss full on her lips. He laughed as she pushed him away. Over his shoulder she saw Alexander standing by the staircase, a glass in his hand, pale as death. The glass fell and shattered – he strode towards them, pulled the mistletoe down, and threw it viciously into a corner.

'It was only Christmas fun, Alex' Anton protested, still smiling. But Alexander hit him (not hard enough to matter) and was shouting unpardonable things. Olivia ran up the stairs and down the corridors, away from the angry voices, to her room, where she threw herself onto the bed, too stunned to find relief in tears. Later there was a knock on the door, and Alexander came in. He sat on the bed beside her. He whispered:

'I'm sorry.'

'You behaved abominably.'

'I've apologised to Anton. He understands.'

'But I don't. Why must you try to spoil our Christmas?

You've been bad-tempered the whole time.'

The room was dark. A shaft of light came in at the door from the hall, the silence was like velvet.

'I love you so much. When I saw him kissing you I couldn't bear it.' She could hardly hear what he was saying:

'Olivia – what's going to happen to us?'

There was no answer to that. She just touched his cheek and said –

'I'm very tired. Go to bed.'

He left, shutting the door softly. Olivia lay there, trembling.

Spring came, and love, which should illuminate and lighten the heart, had plunged Olivia into darkness.

She went to Cambridge for May-week, and stayed at rooms over a baker's shop, chaperoned by Miss Selby. There was a ball every night, picnics at noon, tea-hampers and radios in the punts on the Cam. She danced through three pairs of gold sandals in a week, and was photographed every night – 'A great favourite at the May week dances' said the glossy magazines. Alexander and his friends whirled her through seven mad days and nights – sometimes at three in the morning they would be strung across an empty roadway, moonlight vying with street-lamps, as they sang their way home, to sleep until noon the next day.

It was the last afternoon that Olivia and Alexander went on the river alone. It was a dream of a day, and the newly leafed willows on the bank trailed their pale fingers in the dark green water, the punt hardly making a mark on its surface. They tied up under overhanging branches, the sun dappling down on them. Olivia in a white dress, was lying full length on yellow cushions, with Alexander beside her, propped up on one elbow, looking down at her, his eyes deep and soft. There was a hot smell of new grass, the sleepy lap of water against wet earth. Deliberately, Olivia pulled Alexander down to her, and they lay in close embrace, in their forbidden world.

A few months later, Father Anselm stood on the station platform with Olivia, as they waited for the train to London, where she would begin her journey to Belgium and a convent of an enclosed order. Father Anselm had arranged it all. She had come back from Cambridge ill, afraid, and engulfed in guilt. All she wanted was to escape. No-one knew, of course, except Father Anselm. He had assured her of understanding and forgiveness. She asked for neither. Her parents were shocked by this sudden unlikely decision; and Alexander had bombarded her with letters – Father Anselm said:

'I do not think that it would be wise to answer them. Take care of yourself, my child; tell the Reverend Mother I will visit her soon – and give her this letter from me.' Olivia waved to him from the train window until she could no longer see his solitary figure. Her world receded with every turn of the wheels.

Years passed. Sister Mary Olivia had been a model of obedience, dutiful and immersed in holy teachings. She worked in the garden, in the kitchen, in the laundry. She scrubbed floors and rose at four in the morning, attended every Mass, waited upon the Mother Superior and spent days in utter silence and prayer. The weeks slipped into months, the months into years – time passing unnoticed to the glorification of God.

One day she had a visitor. A solicitor, Pickwickian in shape and manner, came to tell her (she was allowed to receive him in the Reverend Mother's office) that her mother had died, and had left her a large sum of money.

'I have no need of it,' she said sweetly, and at a nod from the Mother Superior added: 'But I will accept it for the convent and its charity school with many thanks.' The solicitor seemed disgruntled, but handed over a paper to be signed. This done, he said:

'Your father and brother send their love, and hope you are well.'

'Tell them I am happy.' And so the little man was bowed out, four heavy doors locked behind him by a succession of silent, soft-stepping nuns.

Alexander had become a writer and lecturer on archaeology. His youthful enjoyment of life had turned to rather soured academic living, although he frequented the Festival Hall and good restaurants. The big house in the country had been sold, and his father had come to live with him in London. Their relationship was on the borderline of mutual distaste – the older man boozy with a liking for cabaret shows on television and plenty of paperback thrillers. He had his own two rooms in the old-fashioned flat which he shared with his son near the Albert Hall. On the desk, where Alexander typed his weekly articles, was the photograph of Olivia in its silver frame; the same one that had overlooked his days and nights in Cambridge. She was still the mainspring of his being – there had been no-one who could open any flood-gates of feeling.

'Rather donnish' said one of his women friends to another. 'No use – but he's not a queer, I'll swear to that. I'll keep on trying!'

It was a bad winter. Alexander's father was ill with bronchitis and covered in shawls and blankets; his room reeked of Friar's Balsam and whisky. One night, when Alexander brought in a hot drink for him, he put down his glasses and his book and said:

66

'I must talk to you. Draw up a chair.'

As the old man sipped his cocoa, he said:

'Listen carefully. And try not to blame me. I am going to break a promise I made to your mother – but I have felt guilty about it all these years, and I have made up my mind.'

Alexander smiled:

'It can't be that important, surely, after all this time? Don't worry yourself – just get better, and rest.'

'That's the point. I'm not going to get better, and I can't rest until we talk.'

'Go ahead, then. I'll give you a sleeping pill later, and you'll have a good night. What is it all about?'

'Olivia.'

'That's a closed book, father.'

'Be quiet.' The old man's voice was harsh. Then he put down his cup, and put his thickly veined hand over his eyes – and began to speak quietly, not looking at his son.

'When you were two years old, your mother was very ill. When she recovered, she was told that she could not have another child. She had miscarried, at six months. It would have been a girl, and we had already given her a name – 'Olivia'. Your mother's depression was so dangerous and deep, that the doctors advised there was only one thing to do. We adopted a baby girl, only eight weeks old, and gave her all the love we had stored up for our own Olivia – she became our own, and your Mother was well and happy again. You and Olivia were never to know. I promised her. I am not going to live long enough to regret breaking that promise. And I love you well enough to tell you; you will know how to deal with it. I think you should have been told – both of you – long ago. It has been hell for me.' The old man was shaking.

Alexander could feel no pity – only a dull anger as

memories rushed through his brain in a raging flood; everything in his childhood swept along in a torrent – the bric-a-brac alongside the uprooted tangle of his world, everything cruelly clear.

They talked freely with each other at last. Alexander sat by his father's bed and held his hand and did not even realise the moment of his going. It was so serene. Days after the death of his father, he decided what had to be done.

At the convent in Belgium, the Reverend Mother received a letter requesting that Sister Mary Olivia be told of the death of her father, and that she be allowed a visit from her brother. These requests were granted and a letter despatched stating the day and the hour. Alexander was ushered into a small ante-room smelling of bees-wax and incense, its bench upholstered in cardinal-red silk, the Crucifix on the wall lit by the up-beam of several candles – a fearful bliss of complete silence: a fly on the window-pane might mean disturbance. From far away, footsteps, shrouded ones, approaching. Alexander stood bare-headed, very thin and tall, waiting. A hatch in the wall opened. Behind a grille of wrought-iron scrolls, he saw the face of Olivia, as white as the linen and cloth of her nun's veiling.

He went close to the grille, and her dispassionate gaze lingered over his face. She smiled, and said:

'Hello, Alexander. You have not changed very much. It is good to see you. Thank you for the letter about father. We said a Mass here for him. It must be lonely for you now. I hope you are taking care of yourself?'

Her voice was cool, emotionless. It matched her face. Alexander was filled with a bitter wish to find her vulnerable, to break this mask into bits, to see the face of the Olivia who had been his.

68

'I have come to tell you something important. It might make a great difference to you. It has to me.'

'I no longer belong to your world, Alexander.'

He saw the white shadow of another nun behind her. So – she was not allowed to talk to him alone; they were free at last – and he wanted to tell her this with joy. He forced himself to have a voice as level as hers had been, but his heart was pounding so hard, it made him short of breath.

'Olivia, you are not my sister. You were adopted when I was two years old. My father promised mother never to tell, but when he was dying he told me. I have all the papers – they were with his will. That is what I have come to tell you.'

Sister Mary Olivia grasped the grille with hands turning white at the knuckles. She swayed a little, and Alexander heard the nun behind her murmur a few words. She stood quite still, radiant, her cheeks flushed, her eyes burning with tears.

'I am so glad. So glad,' she whispered, and looked at him with great tenderness.

'What will happen now? Will you come home to me?'

Sister Mary Olivia's look changed to one of amazement.

'Why do you look at me like that? You know that I love you.' There was a gasp from the little nun in attendance.

'My poor Alexander' Sister Mary Olivia said, 'You must not say this to me. I too have something to tell you. A month ago, I took the final vows. God be with you.'

The hatch was closed quietly and quickly. And the incensed silence was restored.

Eden Rock

In June 1939, the theatres up and down the country were flourishing; Tom Williams was sixteen, just out of school, and had only one thought, one dream, one passion. As he walked beside the sea, he would shout aloud, to the wheeling gulls, scuffing the shingle pebbles with his feet, delighting in the sound of his own voice, a ticket in his pocket for the evening's performance of whatever was on at the theatre. There never was a question in his mind. He would be an actor. He had not told his mother yet, but she would not be surprised. When he had been at school (and to the shop-keepers and neighbours), she had called herself a widow; but now that Tom was grown up, she had told him he could be proud of his father, and that it was all her fault that he had been born out of wedlock. She did not mention who his father was – that was strictly her own business. No wonder he was stage-struck; it was in his blood, and besides this, the last ten years of his young life he had been surrounded by actors in his mother's house by the sea – his grandmother's house, that is – but in her day it had been a respectable boarding-house, they told him. When she died, his mother had made it into very comfortable 'digs' for touring actors, and called it 'Eden Rock' (no-one knew why). The walls were covered with photographs, all nicely framed, with large scrawled signatures praising 'dear Ruby'. Tom had always gone to bed late, and school early. As a pale boy, he sat listening to backstage talk, night after night, his eyes bright, his questions startling the disillusioned mummers who were his mother's paying guests. Sometimes he was allowed into rehearsals – there was usually a new play at the theatre every week. Mrs Ruby Williams would not take 'the musicals', and any vocal or instrumental practice was forbidden within her sacred walls, just as smoking in the bedrooms was. She had once, for a short time, been in the serious drama herself. After three small glasses of port, she might tell about her acting with a great star for a season. Her son was bewitched by the stories she told, and hid a faded photograph of her as 'Ophelia' under his pillow. She was still very pretty at forty, even if she was a bit fat. 'Well-covered and comfortable' she would say, and many a lonely and hungry young actor was nourished by her cosy embraces, as well as her good cooking.

As the gods would have it, Matthew Harding (Now well over sixty), and his Shakespearean company were touring the 'second' dates that spring. He had never sunk so low in his own estimation. Much to his disgust he had to cram his fading, moth-eaten scenery into vans – the cash available was not enough even to cover train freightage – and his company were asked to carry their own costumes. Since the costumes for every play were more or less interchangeable, this was not a major problem.

'Nothing can be a come-down for the true artist,' Matthew boomed to his band of actors gathered on stage for a first rehearsal.

'Give us the great poetry, and our costumes, and maybe only five people in the audience, and we will create magic.' His company groaned, and one of them let fly a four-letter word. There followed a dead silence.

'Would you mind repeating that?'

The young man, who only carried a spear in the second act, apologised, and they all laughed loudly to cover his confusion. Then they trouped out into the warm summer rain to find a bed to sleep in: three of the actors landed at Ruby's 'Eden Rock'; Harding and his leading-lady of the moment stayed at a seedy hotel next to the theatre, and the rest were scattered in various rooming-houses where limp lace curtains hung behind dusty windows. The town was full of early summer visitors, and the company were in high spirits to think that the first night of 'King Lear' would be sold out. Tom was invited by the three who lodged with his mother, to watch rehearsals.

'That old actor,' he told his mother, 'he's not a bit natural.'

'That's the way with Shakespeare, Tom.'

'It shouldn't be.'

'Don't be daft. Mr Harding was marvellous in his day. You're lucky to be seeing him.'

'Did you ever? See him, I mean?'

'Indeed I did. Twenty years ago, at least.' They were in the kitchen and Ruby was ironing shirts. Tom could not see her broken dream in her eyes. Later that morning, when she was sure no-one was in the house, she sat down quietly, to think. What would happen if Matthew found out he had a son? Her son. A kind of exaltation rose in her, half vengeance, half fear, an anticipation of coming events. She felt the years crumble to dust, and trembling, went to the basin to let cold water run over her wrists. In the mirror above it she saw the face of a tired woman, without beauty, no love remaining.

Tom came home in a fever of excitement. One of the actors, the one who was playing Edgar, had lost his voice.

'And guess what! Mr Harding asked me if I would help out and read the part tomorrow. He told me to come back this afternoon after rehearsal, and he'd go over it with me!'

'But you're not old enough. You can't.'

73

'It's only to help; please let me.'

'I'll get him his voice back!' her own voice sounded dark, threatening, like a brooding witch. The voiceless actor was staying in Ruby's house: she would dose him with every known mixture except hemlock, and get him back on stage in three days' time, to save her offspring from misadventure. She could cure any actors' malady, including stage-fright. Tom left half his lunch uneaten, kissed her, and rushed off, leaving Ruby feeling she was in the path of a steam-roller, a confrontation that might destroy her.

In nineteen-twenty, when the South of France still cast a magic spell, Ruby Williams was promised a holiday she would never forget – nor did she.

Matthew Harding was a robust matinée idol famous for his new reading of Shakespeare – triumphant in the lesser classics, and successful in seduction – with no searching eyes of the modern media upon him, he planned his career and romantic adventures without public comment. Only his acting achievements were noted. The fact that he often ended the day rolling and roaring drunk, was only witnessed by his dresser, and the call-boy, back-stage. And of course, by whatever leading lady was breathed upon in a culminating love-scene. Usually, she was so much in love with him that she could not, would not, complain to the management. The management being Matthew Harding himself, it would not have mattered. Ronnie, the poor overworked stage-manager, bore the brunt of cues missed, entrances delayed, and the general anxiety that besets a company when its star misbehaves. They were like a tribe, a family, committed to secrecy and loyalty, if they were to receive wage-packets (very thin ones) at the end of the week. Besides, as it was a touring company, they had a real affection for each other. It often happens in the theatre, where every performance is a joint responsibility, every new production a gamble and a hope, and every audience a question-mark. Every week there were new living-quarters to be found, usually one room each, with a gas-fire, and an inaccessible bathroom, where water-pipes groaned. There would be a 'parlour', where they would find a supper, late at night, left on a large plate, with a cluster of sauce-bottles as a centre piece, and a cloth that by Saturday was splashed with a design of coffee and gravy stains. There was no room or time for jealousy, or mischief, or gossip; they all wore a tough armour, glamour-plated.

Ruby Williams was very young, very tender, when she became leading lady – but only for a while. Matthew Harding taught her a great deal, and seduced her on an uncomfortable red plush sofa in his dressing-room. She went home, sometimes, on Sundays to see her mother, who kept a guest-house in Southsea, and told about her life in the theatre, making it sound much more exciting than it was. She described Matthew Harding as a paragon of an actor-manager, respectful and kind. Mrs Williams always baked a cake for her to take back to him, with her compliments. It was enjoyed by the actors who shared her 'digs', as Harding only relished liquid refreshment and a diet of steak tartare.

For about a month each summer there were no book-ings. In one of these intervals Matthew invited Ruby to travel with him – chaperoned by the long-suffering Ronnie, to keep up appearances. He had been to the South of France (he insisted on calling it 'the Riviera') many times. In his more ebullient days he had stayed at the famous 'Eden Roc' Hotel at Antibes, where exquisite women sunbathed, posing on the slabs of rock like mermaids, in modest bathing suits, only arms and legs exposed to the sun. They had clamoured to meet him, in the bar above the beach, where everyone drank champagne and orange juice for 'elevenses', and a pianist in a rumpled white jacket played the latest Fred Astaire songs, looking sadder and more liverish as the day wore on. In those happy years Matthew had been king of all the galas, a Maharanee offered him sapphire cuff-links, and Mistinguette invited him to Paris. He had always come back to England in need of a rest cure, massage, and a milk diet, before rehearsals could start for a new play.

By the time Ruby came into his life, he was worn out and forgetful, and looked a wreck; but, perversely, that attracted her, because she felt she could refresh him.

Their holiday was spent at a modest pension in Antibes, and they took a bus to Eden Roc every day. Matthew was shameless in telling her how wonderful it all had been. She was very much in love, and Ronnie, the faithful, watched in trepidation, for he knew the pattern of Matthew's affairs only too well. When Ruby told him in confidence that she thought she was pregnant, he begged her not to tell Matthew, bluntly explaining that it would be the one sure way of ending everything. If she had needed proof of Ronnie's theory, she was to get it that evening when she and Matthew had supper at a café overlooking the sea. A young French family at the next table were enjoying themselves enormously. Four children, one an infant, all of them very well behaved, were being given sips of wine, 'Maman and Papa' smiling at each other between loving slaps and attending to bibs, and spoonfuls of mashed potato.

'How revolting,' Matthew said. 'I loathe children. They shouldn't be allowed in public.'

'Would you never want one of your own?' Ruby asked,

as naturally as she could.

'God forbid. Actors must not have families. They are a tie and a hindrance. I should leave any woman who presented me with a child; in fact I have done so in my time.' He leaned towards her, laughing. 'I was married once, Ruby; the infant ended it. Don't look so shocked, my girl. I do not like children or family life. The idea makes me feel ill. Let's change the subject – it's not a problem for us, anyway. Try the lemon sorbet for dessert, it's delicious.'

He did not see the desperate look she gave Ronnie.

Two days after their return, just as rehearsals of the new tour were about to begin, Matthew found a letter from Ruby awaiting him at the theatre. She thanked him for all he had done for her and informed him that, for the present, she would have to give up all thoughts of a career in the theatre as her mother needed her at home. 'Ungrateful little bitch,' he raged at Ronnie, 'after that holiday, too! Get on to that girl who came for an audition a few days ago; red hair and very pretty – her name was Tessa something . . .' Ronnie made a note of it. After a pause Matthew said: 'I could have loved Ruby.'

'I know, sir.'

Matthew Harding sat in his chair on the empty stage. One mean light-bulb lit up the bare boards and snaking cables and ropes; the stalls were covered with dust-sheets, the only sound was the buzz of a Hoover somewhere up in the dress-circle, where a cleaner was trying to draw a fortnight's dust out of a faded red carpet, worn down to patches of grey warp and woof. A hole in the roof allowed some light rain to make a puddle in the middle of the stage. Tom stood in the wings, his heart beating like a hammer, hero-worship blinding him, so that he tripped over a sand-bag. How he reached the centre of the stage he would never know.

'Come on, come on, young man – let's hear you.' Matthew called. He looked magnificent, Tom thought, sitting there like a shabby king, in just the right pose; a wonderful face, like those pictures of the huge stone faces hewn into the rock over in America somewhere. Tom didn't notice the over-long hair lying greasily over a grubby woollen scarf wound twice about his neck, because he wore no collar. He waited for another bidding in that ringing, great voice. Matthew felt the adulation, and reacted as he should.

'Don't be nervous, lad. I was just your age when I had my first audition. Take a deep breath and speak up. This is Ronnie, my stage-manager – he'll cue you.' A small man, thin and grey, came out of the shadows with a script.

'Please Mr Harding, may I do something for you, that I've been learning for a long time – I mean I've been wanting to be an actor always – and you'll tell me if it's no use. Please.' He looked almost like a girl in his eagerness, flushed, with pearls of sweat on his forehead.

'How old are you?'

'Sixteen and a half.'

'That half makes a lot of difference.' Ronnie laughed a little, so Tom took the cue, and managed to smile.

'Well – go ahead. Let me hear what you can do. We've only a few minutes.'

How dared the boy. The old actor heard the first words of Hamlet's advice to the players; he was suddenly alerted, transfixed. For here was a childish prince, his mellow young voice speaking the immortal lines as though he had just thought of them, every cadence a miracle of rightness, something inborn, unteachable, sure and shining.

There was a long silence. A tall shy boy stood there, nervously shifting from one foot to the other. Ronnie blew his nose gustily and broke the spell.

Matthew Harding had heard an echo of himself, a secret spring of a way with words. It was extraordinary. He must not let the boy know how moved he was, so he said sharply:

'Ah, yes. I might find room for you in my company. Only small parts of course, you have a lot to learn.'

I can teach him nothing, nothing. He will flourish and grow, it is all there. It is guidance, an arrow pointing the way; that I can give him. Matthew's thoughts raced into the future. He would have something to live for . . .

'Thank you, Mr Harding. Only . . .'

'What?'

'I'll have to ask my mother.'

'I'll come along and see her, after rehearsal. Ronnie, take the lad's address.'

The actors were coming in, chattering and eating buns. An old stagehand brought benches and chairs, and turned on another arclight. When Tom gave his address – Eden Rock, Marine Parade – Ronnie looked bemused. And Matthew Harding, as he started the rehearsal for 'King Lear' felt grey and stale, and suddenly bereft.

Tom banged the front door shut and yelled 'Mother!' as he came in. Ruby was baking scones in the kitchen, and she took one look at Tom's face and guessed what had happened.

'So what did he say?' but she knew already. 'It's what you want more than anything in the world, isn't it?'

'You know it is. He's coming to see you, to talk about it, after rehearsal.'

'You're not old enough. I would have to sign the contract for you.'

Ruby had to think quickly. It was here, now, the moment she had dreaded.

'Sit down, Tom. There's something you've got to know.'

She told him gently, in a flat voice, that Matthew Harding was his father, and that she had hoped this meeting would never happen.

'And you must go with him, if you want to – and forget as I have, everything that happened, so long ago.'

But Tom hardly heard what she said to him. He was remembering how hard his mother had worked, how much she had loved and encouraged him, and how she had always said he could be proud of his father. Proud?

They did not speak to one another much during that afternoon. He found his mother in his room:

'You'll have to get some new shirts, and maybe another jacket.'

He took her in his arms, and they stood there, holding each other close, the same thoughts unspoken. Then she went and put on her best dress.

Matthew Harding and Ronnie walked briskly along the Marine Parade.

'Eden Roc, did you say? Here we are then, and she spells it with a "k". I'm sure she's never been near the place.'

Matthew was beginning to wonder why he had come. Ronnie could have arranged it; the boy wanted to be an actor, and it seemed unreasonable to have to ask his mother's permission.

They were sitting at the table, having tea and the scones Ruby had baked that afternoon. There had not been a flicker of recognition in Matthew's eyes. This plump, rosy woman in a flowered print dress with house-work hands,

80

pouring tea for them, stirred no memory.

'Your son is very talented, Mrs Williams.' Matthew was using his creamiest voice, 'it would be a loss to the theatre if he were not allowed to be an actor. He reminds me of myself when I was his age – these things are born in one.'

Ruby started to say something, but Tom put his hand over hers and whispered, 'No, mother.'

'Well, my boy, if your mother will just sign the contract we have brought along, we shall see. She need not worry about you – I'll take care you don't get into mischief, eh? Of course, I can't offer you much money –'

The boy had got up and was standing squarely in front of the old actor.

'Thank you, Mr Harding. But I would not go with you if you offered me a million pounds.'

Tom turned on his heel, and with an inherited talent, made a perfect exit.

'It Doesn't Matter, Helga'

Helga Svenson had been with the Robinsons for seven years. She had come over from Norway, the University in Oslo, as an 'au pair', speaking only a few words of English, and looking like a Viking princess. It had been hard work, but she had made herself indispensable; it had taken common-sense, tact, and intense loneliness – but gradually the strain eased, and Edward and Emily became her family. They were middle-aged and mildly adventurous, good-looking and kindly. They tried to find out about Helga's background, but got no further than that her mother and father had been killed in an air-crash when she was an infant – and that she had been brought up by an aunt, and an uncle who drank himself into an asylum. There was a hint of grandparents who had been hunted by the Nazis – but Helga's eyes took on a glazed look when she was asked about her past. So the Robinsons took her as she was, unidentified, even if they never quite got used to her lack of inhibitions. She would dash into the bathroom cheerfully, to bring fresh towels, or ask what was wanted for breakfast, without so much as a quiver of an eyelid, when confronted with either one of them in full frontal display. Then they would remember that on the Norwegian beaches no-one ever wore anything but their own skin.

What Helga could not understand about Emily was her lack of concern or anger for spillage and breakage. Even when three cups from her precious bone china tea-set shattered to pieces as Helga skidded on a small rug, her calm reaction was only:

'It doesn't matter, Helga'.

There were so many disasters at first, that Helga went about the house flushed with remorse. After some months they laughed together, as the mishaps became few and far between. The house in Chelsea was kept in apple-pie order, with good cooking, Edward's shirts beautifully ironed, and that touch of mystery that adds spice to any relationship. They never knew what Helga was thinking, or where she went on her days off – and they were too shy to ask.

In the first year of her stay she spent all her free time exploring, looking into shops and alleyways, with visits to museums, Marks & Spencer's and bus-rides to the City. In the spring she often sat on the bench under the cherry tree blossoming on Chelsea Green, and day-dreamed about the fjords, so oily and opaline at midnight, and the islands, only a boat-ride from Oslo, where seventeen species of mushrooms sprouted under the pines and bilberries carpeted the rocks; but she was not un-happy.

The second phase came later, when she went to night-classes to learn English. One evening, as she was putting her books together, a tall elderly man introduced himself. He was Olaf Krug and he, too, came from Norway – but from the country town of Vinse – that boasted it was the birthplace of Peer Gynt, and an ancient stave church. Helga and Olaf were delighted with each other, despite the differences of age and outlook. He was working in an antique shop owned by an old friend who had emigrated to Britain before World War II. Helga visited the shop, far down on King's Road, among those where the 'antique' business spilled old furniture out onto the pavement, and nobody seemed to sell anything. But sometimes a discerning dealer from the West End would come and browse and buy a thousand pounds worth. Then they would have a party; Olaf and his friend, and old Mr Duffy from the next door shop were all part of this antique circus, and Helga enjoyed her visits to them, and the suppers of herring and black bread and sips of Aquavit. At promptly ten o'clock she would get on a number eleven bus, and be back at the Robinsons' in time to look into the living room where they would be watching television, to say 'I'm back. Goodnight'.

For Christmas that year, the Robinsons gave Helga the money for a holiday in Norway. She decided to wait until the Spring to make use of it, and did not dare to tell them that she really hated the idea of going back to Oslo. She felt thrown into a wilderness, and tossed and turned every night, unable to sleep, trying to imagine where she would go, what she would find. Then a fear began to gnaw at her: perhaps the Robinsons wanted to send her back because she had failed them in some way. Emily noticed the shadows deepening under her eyes, and one morning she came into the kitchen where Helga was shelling peas, and asked her what was the matter.

'Are you ill, Helga? Tell me.'

'O, no. Just a little worried.'

'Do you want to tell me about it?'

At that, Helga collapsed into tears, and Emily put her arms around her and thought how odd it was to see this young woman, usually so nordically unemotional, behaving like a little girl. The peas were scattered on the floor and forgotten, while Helga poured out her sorry story. All the fences were down.

'Of course we want you to stay with us – what a crazy idea of yours! Edward and I were blaming ourselves for being so selfish – for keeping you here so long. Don't you ever want to see Norway again?'

'I suppose so.' She was looking like a mini Garbo.

'You don't seem very sure. Anyway, sweep up the peas; you and I will just have a salad. And we'll have a talk about everything. We both love you dearly – is that understood now?'

Helga looked at Emily and just said,

'Thank you so much. I will not be so foolish again', and proceeded to get pan and brush to sweep up the fresh green peas and put them in the dustbin.

'I have been so wasteful too. It is bad of me.'

'It doesn't matter, Helga.'

That phrase again, so unconcerned; it always gave Helga a shock.

The Robinsons decided that they would take their holiday in Norway too, and Helga would play courier and show them places they would never see on a planned tour. They spent long winter evenings with Helga, trying to learn her language, and she warned them about her country's ethnic habit of fish and cheese and curds for breakfast, and eiderdowns in the bunks in the farmhouse inns, with very little chance of a hot bath. Edward decided to grow a beard, and Emily bought sturdy walking-shoes as heavy as lead. They started saying 'Tak' instead of thank you, and Helga brought in a bottle of Aquavit, and laced their cups of tea with it at bed-time. Altogether a very pleasant manoeuvre.

Helga managed to meet Olaf every week. When he heard she was going to Norway, he was depressed.

'You will not come back.'

'I will! It is only a visit for the Robinsons, and they have invited me. I have nothing to stay there for – you know that.'

One day only a week before the journey, Olaf surprised her with a declaration of love.

'I know I am much too old for you. But if you married me, you would have your own home. The flat above the shop is empty – what do you say?'

'I had no idea you felt anything like that, Olaf. We are such good friends. You have been such a comfort to me.'

'You are trying to tell me you cannot love me. I know I am too old. But I love you very much. I could make you happy.'

'But I *am* happy, Olaf. You are dear to me; but I do not want to marry you or anybody.'

He was sitting in one of the shop's best Georgian chairs, smoking his pipe. 'How grey he looks,' thought Helga – his eyes, his hair, his bulky wool sweater – grey, grey, grey. And his face so deeply lined with kindness. She would never know how much she had hurt him. He felt her eyes upon him and got up quickly and tapped the bowl of his pipe in a brass ash-tray.

'Come along – we'll go to the corner and get a hamburger. Everything's fine as long as you come back to me!' He put his arm around her shoulders – she was tall enough to look straight into his eyes – what she saw there was her own reflection of regret. When she got back to Chelsea that night, she went to her room, and lay on her bed, wide awake for hours.

At the end of May the Robinsons and Helga flew from Heathrow to Oslo. Edward had booked rooms at a small hotel in a back street, and they were given a suite; the large living room high-ceilinged and dark with a heavily framed painting of reindeer on the wall behind a shabby tapestried sofa, a huge oval table in the middle of the room, covered in a dark red cloth, with a fringed lamp hanging low above it. Very Ibsen. The windows were tight-shut and narrow with a lot of dead mosquitoes flattened on the glass – they looked out onto a street with a single track for a cable-tram, that thundered by every hour. The bedrooms were comfortable, but lacking such extravagances as coat-hangers, reading lamps or telephones; the bathroom was a jungle of grey-painted pipes with a huge peeling bath-tub on lion's claws. Emily bit her lip, and said 'Tak' and 'very nice' to the fat proprietor. Edward asked what time was dinner and was told there were no meals to be had except breakfast. 'You should have known' Emily scolded.

The next day things started getting better. The breakfast was stupendous, Edward said: redcurrants stewed with oranges, great bowls of soured milk, smoked fish and heavy bread. Emily winced visibly as she drank her coffee. The sun was shining, and the hired car stood by the curb, waiting, resplendent in red paint, their luggage on its roof-rack, and a smile on its windscreen. Edward took the wheel.

It was a wonderful holiday. Mountains first, then the sea, and finally in among the fjords to the islands, where honey-coloured wild ponies nibbled at the remains of their picnic; swimming among rocks where shrimps tickled their toes – and one day in early July, on the hard blinding snow of a glacier, they watched Helga, on some borrowed skies, come down the mountain like an escaping archangel, haloed in ice.

They spent the last days in Oslo, with a dream behind them, getting used to crowds again, Helga assuring them that everything had changed in seven years. It was strange to hear the blaring pop-music, see King's Road gear, and sense the same mocking patronising mood of the very young, for anyone over twenty. Emily and Edward were ready to go home.

London was basking in sunshine. It took a few days for the Robinsons and Helga to settle down again to their accustomed routine. There was a new facet to their relationship, a glow of something shared and enjoyed, and Helga went about her work with quiet assurance. She thought tenderly of Olaf, and hoped he had received the postcards she had sent; she would surprise him on her first free day. So at the weekend, she boarded the eleven bus, with presents for him in her shopping bag, smiling to herself, knowing how delighted he would be.

The shop door was locked. She peered through the dusty windows and saw no-one. Then went next door, and before she could question old Mr Duffy, he said:

'Ah, Miss Svenson. Sit down. You have heard then?' He peered at her over his glasses. 'I am so sorry. It was a great shock to us all. Three days ago he was quite well, and then . . .' he snapped his fingers. With that sound in her ears, Helga sank into a black void. When she came to, Mr Duffy was making her sip brandy, and she heard herself ask:

'What happened to him? Please tell me.'

Mr Duffy told her how Olaf had fallen down in the shop, and never recovered. His friend had locked up yesterday, and said there would be a cremation service.

'When is that?' Helga whispered.

'Tomorrow. Eleven o'clock.' And Mr Duffy gave her the address of a North-West London crematorium.

'Are you all right now?'

'Yes. I must go. Thank you.' At the door she turned back and gave him the presents she had brought for Olaf. Mr Duffy understood perfectly and held her hand for a moment. Then he took her to the bus-stop a few yards away, and they stood silent, waiting. Helga felt as though all her blood had been drained away and that she was

89

moving in slow motion. When she got on the bus, and it sailed along King's Road she began to see and feel again, and a kind of anger surged in her, almost cancelling grief.

The house was empty – she was glad of that.

When the Robinsons came in, about tea-time, Helga was in the kitchen waiting for the kettle to boil. She had baked scones, and they were piled in a warm pyramid on a plate, jam in a pot, and curls of butter beside them on the tray. Helga was pale and said 'hello' in a shrouded voice.

'What's happened – what's the matter? Why are you back so early?' Edward and Emily crowded in on her, crushing her with worry. So Helga told them in a muted monologue what had happened, and their warm sympathy spilled over. The three of them sat down at the kitchen table, Emily holding Helga's hand, and Edward pouring the tea. They had heard very little about Olaf Krug before this. So now Helga had to tell them the whole story, and they were surprised, sorry, and a little shocked, but said all the right things and made her feel much better.

'Of course you will go to the funeral tomorrow,' Emily said.

'You think I must?'

'But surely you want to? You are the only one who cared about him.'

'I suppose so. Do I have to wear black?'

'No, dear. But wear a hat.'

'I do not have a hat.'

Emily said: 'I'll lend you one. I must have one somewhere.' And she buttered another scone. It was all very comforting.

Next morning Emily brought the promised hat to Helga's room. It was old fashioned, round and flat, made of hair straw, its brim covered by a circle of white silk roses set snugly one against another.

'I used to wear it for Ascot.' Emily watched Helga try it on. 'It looks lovely on you.' And indeed it did, perched on Helga's shoulder length blonde hair. When she put on her black raincoat, she looked quite ready for the solemn occasion.

Edward had ordered a taxi, and paid the driver to take Helga to the crematorium, and to wait for her, and bring her back safely. She had no idea what it would be like. When she arrived there, she was asked whom she had come for, as though she was trying to gate-crash a party. Her heart was thumping as she gave Olaf's name, and was taken to a dark room next to the chapel. An old usher told her that a service was still going on for someone else, and that she was to wait. She sat down on a hard wooden bench, like a church pew.

A clock on the panelled wall was ticking loudly, and she heard faint organ-music. It was very hot, and she took off her hat and put it on the bench beside her – she would put it on again when they called her. She leaned back and closed her eyes.

She did not hear the old usher come into the room. He looked at her through thick lenses, and then saw a wreath of roses on the bench beside her. He took it up tenderly and tiptoed out again. The next thing she knew was that a minister opened the door and said: 'A friend of Mr Krug? This way please.' The organ music was still playing, the clock had ticked for only five minutes, and she realised she must have dozed. She reached for the hat. It was gone. She had no time to think, or ask, or even care. The chapel was lovely. No-one was there. Candles were alight and the coffin was raised on a platform; the young minister standing behind it, staring down in disbelief at its floral tribute; then he collected himself, and addressed his holy words to the one person in the chapel. The organ-music swelled, the curtained trap-door opened and the coffin slid noiselessly away, Emily's white Ascot roses, and Helga's chance of a life and a love of her own, turning to ashes.

She knew exactly what Edward and Emily would say: 'It doesn't matter, Helga'.

Prima Donna

In Tuscany, the sunlight is sifted gold, turning the stone and stucco of old houses to flushed beauty. The shadows are long and purple – the people short and sun-burned, with strident voices like young ravens – the exceptions being when they sing like nightingales. One of these was Emilia Franchi, who trilled her way through a few years of village schooling, and factory, into the opera houses. Every minor town in Italy boasts of its grand opera, offering opportunities for budding Pavarottis and Frenis. It is better not to mention the particular town where all this happened, because perhaps Emilia and Enrico and Roberto are still there, and all the people who caused the trouble, too.

To begin with, Emilia worked in a small glove factory. She, and a hundred other girls sat stitching fine leather, glacé kid and suede in jewel colours; and coarse pig-skin and yellow chamois in large sizes for the gentlemen who frequented the race-courses and casinos. In the evenings after work, Emilia went home to her parents (her father was a worker in wrought-iron), and seven sisters and brothers in varying states of childhood and adolescence. She would not eat the great heaps of pasta, for she dreamed of sequin dresses and a figure like Lollabrigida's. All those nibbles of garlic and slices of onion might be good for her voice, but would certainly not encourage suitors. The one thing they all agreed upon, was her determination to become an opera-singer. It was almost as admirable as being a nun, and much more profitable. So she was cossetted, as the family investment should be.

The glove factory was owned by 'Perini Fratelli' or vice versa. Only the Fratelli (Brothers) didn't exist – there was no brother, only a son. But 'Fratelli' looked better printed on the white and gold labels sewn into every glove. Roberto Perini was a large amiable man, very rich, very Catholic, and a doting father. His son, Enrico, was not good-looking or clever, and was rather backward with girls. When he was twenty-one, he was put into the factory as floor-manager. This was a delightful occupation, overseeing a hundred girls making beautiful gloves, in a great loft whirring with little sewing-machines, and smelling of expensive leather, cheap perfume, and perspiration.

One day, during the lunch-hour, some of the girls were sitting in the sun as usual, on the stone balustrade outside the door in the courtyard. They sat in a line, swinging their legs in bright skirts (no trousers allowed by Mr Perini) eating oranges and talking and twittering for all the world like a flock of birds resting from a migration flight. Suddenly, one voice rose above the rest – high notes stabbing the noon-day, and the chattering was hushed. At that very moment, Enrico rode into the courtyard on his bicycle, and paused, riding high on one foot, as a note, pearly and pure, hung in the air and trailed to a stop. The girls giggled as he bent, very properly, to remove the bicycle clips from his tight trousers.

'Who sings like that?' he asked no-one in particular.

'Emilia,' answered a chorus of voices.

'Emilia who?'

'Franchi.'

'Bring her to me.'

Three girls went to find her. She was eating a piece of

sausage and washing it down with coca cola.

'The boss wants to see you.'

'Jesu Maria! What for? I haven't done anything wrong!' She wiped her mouth, and took a little mirror out of her apron pocket.

'I look terrible.'

In fact she was extremely pretty. Her brown hair tied back with a piece of string, no make-up on her shining face, and eyes large and limpidly amber, her mouth a curve of smiles. There were several other important curves to be seen under her thin blouse and flowered skirt. At this moment she was scared – she tried to think if she had made a mistake – perhaps packed two left-hand gloves as a pair, or maybe the boss had found out about that snippet of violet suede she had taken – it hadn't been enough to use at the factory, so she had taken it home and made a little mat to put under the fruit bowl. She would offer to pay for it. By the time she reached Enrico, standing by his bicycle, she was in a state of nerves. She twisted her cotton skirt in her fingers and did not look up at him. The other girls retreated, looking back over their shoulders, wondering. When Emilia finally looked at him, Enrico was smiling, and his eyes, black as shoe-buttons, had laughter in them. She felt faint with relief.

'You wished to see me, Sir?'

'I heard you singing. It is a very fine voice.'

'Thank you, Sir. I do not sing except at the lunch-break. I am sorry if I have done anything wrong.' At that moment a piercing bell called all the girls back to their work-benches, and suddenly the courtyard was quiet and empty, like a hive whose bees had swarmed. Enrico stood lost in thought; he leaned his bicycle against the wall and climbed up the outside staircase to his office which looked over red roofs to the golden dome of the cathedral. There

95

was not much to do; the same orders year after year, doubled in the tourist season. But now it was early spring, and nowhere in the world can spring be so full of promise, so burgeoning, so physical, as in Tuscany. Emilia's voice rang in Enrico's ears and he longed to hear it again; how splendid, he thought, if one day a great soprano could say that she had been discovered in the Fratelli glove factory.

On the work-bench Emilia was dreaming too. What a sweet little man, she said to herself. Like an overgrown cupid, all round and rosy. If he could grow a moustache, he would be quite presentable.

That evening, after supper, Enrico told his father about Emilia and her wonderful voice. Roberto Perini was popping grapes into his mouth, and swallowing them, pips and all, as he listened indulgently to his son. He said:

'If you are really serious about this vocal miracle, bring her to see me, and I'll get the music-master from the Conservatorium to come and hear her, too. And then we will see. It is a big responsibility to have a protegée. And her family may make trouble. Perhaps it would be wise if you went to see them before we decide. Take it slowly, my son. It is maybe that love is blurring your vision.' And he patted Enrico on the shoulder.

Enrico did not feel like being patted – his manhood had risen to a high level. Next day and every day he managed to watch Emilia, and she knew he was watching; and at last one evening he waited at the factory gate until she came out.

'May I walk home with you?'

She had expected this for days, so of course she agreed, and he was invited in to meet her family, who had all been expecting him too. It was an overpowering experience for Enrico who lived alone with his father. They were all quite polite to him, but after he had gone, having clicked his heels, and kissed Mama Franchi's hand, Emilia was put on the rack.

'Have you been flirting with him?'

'No, papa.'

'Has he made any improper suggestions?'

'No, papa.'

The family were puzzled. But delighted when Emilia was invited to the Perini house to sing for the music-master. He assured Roberto and Enrico that they had found a jewel, who would one day sing at La Scala, (but that it would take years to prepare her). Roberto felt that at last Enrico had shown some sense, and wrote a letter to Emilia's father, asking for his permission to send her to a famous singing teacher in Florence. He would arrange with a very respectable spinster relative to take her as a boarder, and of course she would come back to her family every weekend. He considered it an honour, he wrote, to be able to foster such a talent, and he was sure Emilia would prove worthy of the trouble and expense. Also, he hoped that they would look favourably upon his son, Enrico, who was devoted to their daughter.

The Franchi family could hardly believe their luck. So everything settled into a hectic routine for the summer. Emilia blossomed with self-importance and moved to Florence where the Perini aunt fed her well, saw that she got to bed early and did not hang over her balcony watching the crowds strolling along beside the Arno. She was taken to the opera once a week to learn, not to enjoy. The 'famous' singing teacher was enchanted, but worried. Her voice was not remarkable as yet, and she was just a little stupid. A country girl with a lovely complexion and a trusting nature, and a small round bosom that took his mind off her vocalises as it rose and fell with her intake of breath. It was more than he could bear when he had to put his hand on her diaphragm and say 'Push', so that her coloratura would have a firm base. Ah! well, he was almost eighty and deserved a thrill. He had a great many pupils, sophisticated, fashionable, and some opera singers who still came to him with their vocal chords in trouble. So Emilia was his ewe-lamb, and he was determined to make her into a Prima Donna. 'Prima' he would say, rolling the R like a drum, 'must mean what it says: first and best.'

Enrico wooed her at the weekends. She found it hard to readjust to her family, even though she knew how much they loved her. The evenings with Enrico and his father were more to her taste now, with silver on the table, and at least two courses served rather grudgingly by their housekeeper. No heaps of pasta here, or easy laughter. Enrico had lost a lot of weight, and was almost good-looking, and old Roberto (he was only fifty) beamed at them both and taught Emilia all about wine, and how to use the telephone, and how to raise her eyebrows when she was displeased. Roberto could answer every question she asked – and there were many. So . . . after a year, Enrico and Emilia were affianced. There was a reception which lasted eighteen hours, and Emilia was given a large amethyst ring, and her family were all there, uncomfortable in their best clothes, sitting on little gold chairs. In the evening, Enrico's friends took him to a high-class brothel, which was supposed to celebrate the end of his bachelorhood; and Emilia went back to her studies in Florence, the amethyst glowing on her finger, and a fatherly kiss from Roberto on her brow.

The next year she was almost ready for her opera debut. It was decided that when she married Enrico, there would be no children until her career was established. He agreed to this, for his marriage to Emilia was after all one of great pride and deep devotion. (Besides, he had a mistress by

98

now, who had already borne him a daughter.) As for
Emilia, all her sex was in her singing. She felt like a tree,
breathing deeply, her feet apart, planted firmly on the
ground, the sap and energy flowing upwards to the
orgasmic floating and flooding of high notes, the elation,
the fulfilment, the relaxed fatigue – all, she was sure, gave
her more pleasure than would a night in bed with Enrico.
But she had to keep her side of the bargain. So they were
married, in the Cathedral; all the girls from the glove
factory were invited and given a bonus and three pairs of
gloves – and Emilia's father wished secretly that she was
marrying some nice country boy. There was no honeymoon, and she went to live in Roberto's house.

'La Traviata' was chosen for Emilia's first appearance.
She suffered agonies of self-consciousness at the endless
rehearsals. The opera people were very kind and helped
her along – they were all used to awkward new singers
taking up their time, performing once or twice, never to be
seen or heard of again. They were tolerant and encouraging (for was she not the pupil of the greatest singing
teacher?) and they had to admit she was talented, and so
they called her 'Bambina'. Elsa Correnti, the leading
soprano, taught her how to make up – and was startled to
see she had turned a country prettiness into extravagant
beauty. Enrico came to some rehearsals, and in the
evening she would hurry back to Roberto's house, sit on
Enrico's knee until it was time for him to tuck her into bed.
He would then hurry to a secret address and the arms of
his amenable mistress.

One day during rehearsal, Enrico was called into the
foyer. A small man, in an alpaca suit, rings on his fingers,
and a black felt hat set rakishly over one of his red-rimmed
eyes, was waiting for him.

'Signor Perini?'

'Yes.'

'The husband of the new soprano?'

'What do you want to see me about?'

'Your wife. She is to sing here soon, is she not?'

'Yes – in "Traviata", next month.'

'Exactly. Perhaps you do not realise sir, all that that entails.'

'I don't understand what you are talking about.'

'You see, we can make her a great success, or we can do the opposite.'

The man was smiling and rubbing his hands as though he was using soap.

'Explain yourself.'

'You have heard of the "clacque" of course?'

'No.'

'But everyone knows about us! Some of the leading singers use us – when the new ones begin and they are too poor to pay they just disappear – quickly – unless they are a Callas or a Pavarotti.'

'What are you telling me this for?'

'A small fee will ensure lots of applause and Bravos for your wife.'

'This is disgraceful – how dare you suggest it to me! – my wife will stand on her own merits. Does the Opera House know about all this?'

'But yes! Your wife need not know about it, Signor Perini. She will just have the joy of successful appearances. Otherwise I am afraid . . .' the man shook his head sadly, 'the audience might sit on their hands – and the critics will take their cue from that, no matter how good she is. And that would be a very sad thing, would it not?' He pushed his pock-marked face nearer to Enrico. 'Think it over. When is the debut?'

'In three weeks' time.'

'Ah. There is time to gather some good men. We will place them all over the house – but mostly in the gallery. If you want flowers thrown onto the stage it will cost a bit more. But it adds a lot to the gala feeling. And we can guarantee at least five solo curtain calls.'

He sounded like an undertaker. Enrico was appalled. The man mistook his silence for approval.

'We can make it most unpleasant also. We can shout bad words at the singer and force an exit. But we have only done this a few times – it is against our principle, Signor. I promise you your wife will find herself a great success. I congratulate you. I will call on you next week, and I'm sure we will come to an agreement. Good day to you.'

And he scuttled down the broad steps of the opera-house, and was lost in the mid-day crowd. The man in the box office was laughing.

'Caught you, has he?'

'Do you know him?'

'Know him? Dirty little blackmailer. We've had him around for years. Sometimes couldn't do without him. He'll cost you a pretty penny, though. I've seen singers ruined, no matter how good they are – he takes most of their salary. If he wanted to, he could close this opera-house in a week. The police can't do anything. Don't tell your wife anyway.'

'This is ridiculous. I must see the manager at once.'

'If I may suggest, Sir, that would be unwise. You are lucky you have not been asked to subscribe to your wife's debut.'

Enrico shrivelled where he stood. Because he suddenly remembered paying a large sum some months before to procure a dresser for his wife, help with costumes, and a fund for the orchestra. So he was caught up already. He wondered if his father knew that this kind of thing went on. Or maybe Emilia herself knew about it. He thought of all the performances there, and the enthusiasm, the Bravos, and Elsa Correnti bowing, clinging to the velvet curtain, being pelted with flowers. Was it all miserable fixing and make-believe? As he walked away, the man in the box office leaned out of his cubby-hole and laughed.

'How many seats would you like for "Traviata" Signor Perini? There are only a few left – the public is very curious about new prima-donnas.'

Enrico felt as though an arrow had pierced him between the shoulder blades. On no account must Emilia ever know about this. He would fork out the money and would say nothing about it, even to his father. After all, it would not hurt anyone if the applause was over-enthusiastic. And suppose, just suppose, (he squirmed at the idea) Emilia was not as talented as he thought she was? Suppose all those lessons and years of work had been for nothing? Worse than that, suppose her teacher had tricked him – suppose his own father had ulterior motives, suppose – suppose? His suspicions came to a full stop as he thought of Emilia's warm affection and lovely voice. But the poison had entered his veins. Nothing was the same now. Despite his agonising thoughts, he managed to treat Emilia like a precious jewel, he was even more encouraging, more considerate. In utter disgust he handed a fat roll of bank notes to the little man in the black felt hat, and promised him the remainder before the first performance. He went to the last rehearsals, and found there were things in Emilia's singing he did not like, which he had not noticed before. She scooped some high notes and stood with her feet apart, and her low notes were too heavy. After all, Enrico thought, if a man is paying for something, he becomes more critical, he expects perfection. By the end of the dress rehearsal, he was convinced that if it were not for the paid 'clacque' and the little man's secret army, Emilia might be, indeed would be, a sad failure. So he breathed freely, convinced now that he had saved her – and himself – from humiliation. He was feeling exceedingly unwell as he let himself into the house that evening. The next day he woke late, and when Claudia, the housekeeper, found him he was trying to dress himself, and she knew he had a raging temperature. 'Influenza', she thought, and pulled his trousers and shirt off (she was used to putting him to bed since he was a little boy). The tension and worry suddenly overwhelmed him, and he burst into tears. She brought him a hot drink, and went to telephone the doctor. Emilia was told not to go into his room, of course – and his father was dismayed to find Enrico frantic, tossing about in bed, his temperature rising, complaining of a little man leering at him from the bed-post, and talking wildly. Roberto tried to calm him, and told him he would report every detail of Emilia's debut that night; at that Enrico clutched his father's arm, saying that Emilia would be booed off the stage, and that tomatoes and bad eggs would be thrown at her. Roberto laughed, and then Enrico gave a great groan and buried himself in the pillows and bedclothes. His father had heard of men having pains when their wives were in labour, but this transmission of stage-fright was ridiculous.

Emilia sat in her dressing room at the opera-house, making up her face. She was distressed about Enrico. She sipped soda-water from a glass; and then sang a scale to be sure that two and half octaves of notes were in order. It was still two hours till curtain-time. An eternity. There was a knock at the door.

'Come in, the door is not locked.'

A little man came in and stood twirling a black felt hat in his hands, looking sheepish.

'Who are you? What do you want?'

'I am come about the money from Signor Perini. He was to give it to me before the performance.'

'What money? What are you talking about. Signor Perini is very ill and will not be here tonight. I hope he will be well in a few days. Surely any business can wait?'

The man was obviously upset and embarrassed.

'But all these men – they expect payment. You do not know about the transaction, then?'

'What men? What is it about?'

So, very carefully and politely, the man explained that Enrico had not meant her to know; and fury rose in her. She got up and strode up and down the small dressing room. Then suddenly she became very quiet and spoke to him slowly, as though he were a delinquent child:

'Listen to me. If you managed to frighten my husband into thinking I'd be a failure, you'd better think again. I ask you to tell those rats of yours that I wish to know exactly what the audience thinks of me, even if it means I never sing again. I'll make a bargain with you: tell your men to go home and take their bravos and their dirty hands with them. How many are there?'

'Twelve.'

'What do twelve empty seats matter? And if – no, when I am a success tonight, you have my word I will pay you double that which my husband promised you.' She was in great form now, and grinned at him.

'But send in the flowers you were going to pelt me with. I'll wear one to remember you by. Now get out, you poor wretch. You'll get your money tomorrow – get out.' She took him by the shoulder and pushed him through the door and banged it so hard that it almost caught the tail of his coat.

So. Enrico did not believe in her. She would never

forgive him. Adrenalin, rage, were pouring into her veins, in waves of exultation and energy – as she waited to go on stage. She sang as she had never sung before, a new dimension to a musically perfect performance, and the audience, silent at first, went wild, and shouted and applauded, and smothered her in flowers – even the conductor put down his baton and blew her a kiss, before he motioned the whole orchestra to stand up and applaud. And Emilia? As she bowed again and again in front of the red velvet curtain, she had no feeling of achievement – it was only what she had always expected of herself, since she dreamed it in the glove factory.

Old Roberto came into her dressing room, looking so handsome in white tie and tails, his face glowing with pride under an opera hat. He enveloped her in a huge unfatherly embrace, 'Brava, Prima Donna!'

Fantasia

Once a week she sat at the same table in the window of the tea-shop opposite his office. He never had time for tea, but this was more than he could bear, and he decided that he would arrange somehow to finish work at four o'clock on Fridays. Her beauty from that distance seemed magical; he told himself he would be disillusioned if he went nearer, but he had an overwhelming desire to see her at close quarters, to hear her voice; but perhaps, he told himself, her eyes had a squint, perhaps she stuttered or lisped, or her nails were bitten to the quick.

He half-shut the venetian blind of his office-window, and sat down behind the raised drawing-board. He was an architect, a designer, a creator of lines and arches and long vistas, and the stretch of his imagination was infinite. He had never found perfection in man, beast or building; he had never been in love. He read about crime, wars, poverty and corruption every day, and washed them out of his mind as easily as he washed the charcoal and blue ink off his fingers before he walked back to his lodgings every evening. By that time the tea-shop would be tight shut, a net spread over the left-over pastries on the window-ledge.

Two months before, he had been sent to this place, little more than a village, from a large firm in London. They considered it a major assignment for him to become head designer in their country branch, which specialised in the restoration of beautiful but decaying houses for miles around. He was still in the process of daily discovery – he knew only his fellow-workers, the postman, and his landlady. So that, this vision every Friday, of a beautiful young woman alone, drinking tea and gazing out of the window of the tea-shop with mournful eyes (he was sure it must be so), was quite enough to raise his passionate curiosity.

This particular Friday afternoon was an enchantment, as an April day can so easily be in England. He felt miracles could happen. At four o'clock he opened the door of the tea-shop, heard a small peal of bells, and breathed in a delicious smell of toasted muffins and faint chocolate. It seemed crowded – but it was a small space and only a few elderly people murmured gently to each other, the clink of their cups touching their saucers politely. An eager thin lady came towards him: 'Good afternoon Sir, would you mind sharing with someone?' She led him straight to the table in the window where Jenny was pouring her tea.

They did not talk much. They were shy and suspicious of one another. She said her name was Jenny Bolton, and that she came to shop in the village once a week and have her tea, and that she always had to leave before five o'clock. He said: 'I know that', and told her he was David Macguire, and that he had been watching her from his office window across the street. She laughed at him, and even that laughter matched his pre-dreaming of her. She was lovely, a fair transparent skin, a wing of silky blonde hair swept upwards from a smooth forehead and dark grey eyes; a small childish voice, bolstered by great eagerness to talk, and yet he felt a great reticence about her.

'Have you lived here always?' he asked.

'For about twelve years.' Her eyes clouded over. 'I think.' She smiled.

That 'I think' worried him. Something told him to ask no questions. She would tell him what she wanted to – and

108

no more. She seemed to have no curiosity about him, but he talked about himself, of course, without her asking.

'Beautiful houses?' she enthused, 'How wonderful to be able to restore them! I've lived in so many. All over the world.'

David was surprised. 'You are very young to be able to say that.'

'My parents take me everywhere . . . Everywhere . . .' Jenny's voice trailed – then very brightly: 'I'll tell you all about it. But I must go now.'

She got up, and he helped her to put on her jacket. It was like touching a bird, brittle vulnerability under softness. When he said:

'Next Friday, then?' she turned at the door and nodded. He sat down at the table again, and watched her get on a bicycle and ride away. His tea had gone cold, and the customers had long since gone.

During the week David enquired at the office if anyone knew of a family called Bolton. Nobody did. Nor was the name in the small list of householders in the post office directory. So he imagined Jenny was living with friends – he would soon find out, he promised himself. He worked with fiendish energy all the week, and by four o'clock on the Friday there was nothing on his mind but the meeting with Jenny. He felt she was already his own; he could recite her face like a poem and her voice lived in his inner ear; his limbs ached with love but he gave this condition no name or recognition, any more than the tears which sprang so easily to his eyes on these clear spring mornings, when he thought of Jenny.

The fussy thin lady of the tea-shop was overwelcoming as David came in, and brought a dish piled high with cream cakes. As she leaned over their table with the steaming tea-pot, David caught a whiff of lavender, and a wisp of her straying grey hair brushed his cheek, like a moth. She looked at them both as though she shared a joyful secret and disappeared through a green baize door.

Then came the ritual of tea between them, shy and rather clumsy. Milk – no milk? No sugar – two sugars; no, nothing to eat. Thank you.

'Do you smoke?' asked Jenny.

'No. I never liked it enough.'

'My father smokes, those long thin beautiful cigars. He looks so handsome in his white summer suit and Panama hat. Very sunburned.'

'Not in England, surely?'

She laughed: 'No-no, when I was little we were in South America. Mother wore long white lace dresses. And used a parasol. She tied a big bow in my hair that matched my sash. O, I was happy!'

'Where are your parents now?'

Her eyes were bright.

'They're away. I'm waiting for them here. I was ill, you see, and they went on travelling without me. But before that, I've been all over the world with them. Russia, and Bali, and even Japan. I still have a doll they bought me there. Imagine!'

'I can't imagine. I've only been to Paris and Venice.'

'O, Venice! There was a man there, who took me in his gondola. He had a black moustache and smelled of tuberoses.'

To David, who was sure all Italians smelled of garlic, this came as a revelation.

'My parents hurried me away.'

'I don't wonder.'

Jenny laughed again and leaned towards him and put her hand on his. He withdrew it, like a snail into its shell, and then wished he hadn't. She asked:

'Have you ever been in love?'

'I don't know.'

'O, but you would know, if you had been.'

'Have you?'

'Lots of times. More tea?'

'No thank you.' David looked at her – she was flushed and more beautiful than he had imagined. And older. Something in her alerted all his senses. She was the Lorelei, Melisande, Heloise, and Scheherazade.

'Tell me more about you' was all he could find to say.

'My life is wonderful. Father is very rich, you see. He writes travel books. When I was a child there were horses and cars and yachts. And lots of people. I was too young to know how important they were – and some of them were quite horrid.'

'And your mother.'

Jenny's voice sounded distant and small. 'When she kisses me it's like rose-petals falling.'

'Don't tell me about it if it makes you unhappy.' They drank their tea in silence. Then he asked her:

'Where did you go to school?' 'A convent, of course, whenever we settled anywhere. The nuns didn't mind how little I knew, or where I'd been before. They taught the same things in each convent. Anyway I am very stupid.'

'You seem to know quite enough.'

'I read a lot. I must learn to knit – it will pass the time.'

'But you have friends here?'

'Of course, I'm staying with them. They're lovely people – but no-one like you. I can tell you things.'

'It's the same with me. I feel I've known you always. I've thought about you for days.'

'I'm not worth that. Please don't.'

'You must let me meet your parents when they come back.'

'Why?'

'They sound fascinating.'

'They are. Father knows about everything. Mother plays the piano beautifully. She studied with a great musician – Rubinstein, I think.' Jenny frowned, a funny criss-cross between her eyes that could not be taken seriously.

'How thrilling,' David said. 'I didn't know Rubinstein ever gave lessons.'

'Perhaps he doesn't.'

'Not any more, anyway; he's dead.'

'O? Mother will be sorry. Perhaps we had better not tell her.' David felt bewildered, incapable of thinking straight. He said:

'Music means a lot to you?'

'Yes. I had a violin once, but I don't know where it is now. When they come back, my parents, they'll put everything in order, you'll see.' She smiled.

'I look forward to that.'

'We went to New York for a whole year – and when we came back, I was ill – I told you.'

'New York must be marvellous.'

'It was noisy. I liked the Zoo, in the park. In the place where some deer were caged, there was a square pond of water with a sign on it: "Water-hole". As though the deer could read! They are funny, the people over there. The buildings are so tall, everybody looks like a midget, like the circus. From up high, the traffic looks like little toy cars. I used to watch from the hotel window.'

'But the blue and bronze glass sky-scrapers must be terrific – we only have one or two in Britain!'

'Blue glass?' Jenny looked puzzled.

'Forty or fifty storeys high – you couldn't miss them. A crystal city. Fire and ice!' David's vision made him laugh with joy. Jenny looked at him in amazement.

'You're making it up!'

'No – no – bankers and businesses have built those fantastic monsters – how could you possibly miss seeing them?'

Jenny withdrew from this onslaught. She seemed to sink within herself.

'I was in the park mostly, feeding the squirrels. The most glittering thing I saw was the statue of General Sherman blazing gold in the sunshine, opposite the hotel where we stayed.'

David was enchanted by her indifference – he wanted to see the world with her, to embrace her, hoard her beauty, clamp her to himself. He watched her lips move as she rambled on about her fragmented travels. She chattered about endless cruises, ski-holidays, and a flat in Paris. David came back to full attention.

'They left me in a convent there for several months. Then father came for me, and we went to Italy. New York came later.'

'Did you fly in the Concorde?'

'Fly?' Jenny looked puzzled. 'Never-never.'

'Concorde, the millionaire's way to travel.'

'We always went by ship. Those gorgeous big ones. Caviar every day. And those great swans sculptured in ice, with coloured lights inside, at the Captain's dinner.'

'But surely, you flew . . .'

Jenny stared at him and jumped to her feet. Her whole personality seemed to change – she looked tortured, trapped. Just then a large shining Limousine stopped across the road.

'I'm late. I must go. No – don't come with me.' She put

her hand on his arm. 'They mustn't know I meet you here.' She reached up and kissed him swiftly on the cheek; and then darted out of the door and ran across the road. He saw her talking hard and fast to a tall woman who got out of the car, and put her arm around Jenny's shoulders. A liveried chauffeur held the car-door open. Then it slid noiselessly away, and David stood in the door of the tea-shop, bereft.

'We're closing now,' the tea-shop lady twittered behind him.

'See you next Friday?'

'Oh, yes.' And he went out.

As she closed the door, she noticed Jenny's bicycle outside, leaning against the bay-window. She opened the door again and called to David.

'Mr . . . Mr . . .' He turned.

'Maguire.'

'Please, Mr Macguire, perhaps you would take Jenny's bicycle back to her? She's staying at Bede Manor, only three miles from here – you know.' She said 'You know' with such assured implication that he nodded wisely, as if, of course, he knew. It was evidently a show place, this home of Jenny's friends. He was thrilled to think he would find her there.

David wheeled the bicycle with one hand through the country lanes. They were as quiet as cathedral aisles in the late sunshine, and in some stretches as highly arched by beech and oak and ash. In the soft quiet he could even hear the flutter of a bird's wings from tree to tree. Only the hum and throb of a low-flying plane brought him back to here and now. At a turn in the lane he came upon a gate. It was at least twelve feet high, of iron-work, gilt embellished, between two mossy stone pillars each with a weathered urn on top, overflowing with ivy. Beyond he could see a meadow and lawns like velvet, and a large house, rambling, old and mellowed, its brick turning to deep rose in the setting sun. As his hand reached up to push the gate, something gleamed in the sunlight. It was the gold lettering on a boarded sign at the gate-post:

'Bede Manor. Home for the Mentally Disturbed.'

*   *   *

From the Times, London, January 1965:

'It is now known that Reginald Bolton, the travel author, and his wife were among those killed in the New York to London air crash last week. Their thirteen-year-old daughter is among the survivors.'

Entente Cordiale

Laura had always wondered why her Aunt Fabienne had never married. There was an aura of romance about her, something perfumed, a smile that hinted at unforgotten adventures and a loveliness undimmed. Her hair still had streaks of gold, and her eyes, retreating now into the protection of heavy lids, were of a deep violet-blue. They gazed at you hungrily, Laura thought – enviously perhaps, yet in tune with all things new and young; she used a gold-rimmed lorgnette to read, and a silver knobbed ebony cane when she walked – otherwise the years had left her uncluttered. She was still always dressed by the house of Chanel – and when she showed Laura old photographs, it seemed nothing about her had changed very much. The yearly visit to Paris had always been happy for Laura. Fabienne's flat overlooking the Seine, flowing lazily towards the Île St Louis. The rooms did not have the shadowy ambience that the elderly sometimes insist upon. In summer it was full of bright colour, and sunlight and air. In winter the curtains would be drawn, and lamp-light and fire-light vied with each other, making everything deeper, even the red of the roses in the green glass vase.

They spoke French together always. Fabienne's sister had married a Scot, and Laura had been born in a small town on the Border, and gone to Edinburgh University. Her parents had not been too pleased when she started the visits to Paris; but she was over thirty now, with a degree and a professorship in psychology, and her life was ordered as she wished it to be. She thought of her parents as rather backward children. They had never got over the shock of her 'living with' her doctor-friend when she was at university, without a thought of marriage. There had been no rift – but self-consciousness fell upon them like a pall, and in an argument about the situation one Sunday at lunch, years ago, her mother had let several cats out of the bag when she cried: 'Just look at what's happening to poor Fabienne!' At that time, Laura wondered.

A fresh Spring morning. Fabienne opened her eyes and saw the net curtains billowing inwards, heard sounds of the barges already on the river, and a pair of sparrows chattering on her balcony railing, evidently a lover's quarrel, their feathers puffed and ruffled, hopping in fury, waiting for the crumbs that they knew would come their way from Fabienne's breakfast. She stretched her arms above her head, and then pushed her legs, till her toes touched the brass rail at the bottom of her bed: Lili would knock in a moment and come in with her breakfast. She waited for this moment with joy and appetite. Coffee steaming in a Sèvres pot, (never in metal, of course), warm croissants in a basket, covered with a fine linen cloth, the morning's letters, and 'Le Matin' – a newspaper potpourri of world events. Sometimes articles on a book, or a play to be read, letters, bills. And always the blue envelope from London – addressed in that firm small hand that was like a whispered word in her ear, reassuring her that all was well.

Lili had been with her for years – they had been through World War II together when they were girls, united classlessly in the Resistance just before the Nazis walked into Paris; when it was over, Lili insisted on staying close, to serve her in any way she could. It was Lili who comforted her when Andrew was reported missing, and rejoiced with her on the day he suddenly rang the door-bell, bedraggled, returned from prison-camp to take her in his arms. He had spent a month with her in Paris, and then had to go back to London to take up the threads of his work in the Foreign Office. Fabienne had never known what that work was; only that it was important, part politics, part finance, and that she must keep a low profile for his sake. He had never told her this, but she knew it instinctively. There were periods when he didn't come to Paris for months at a time – it had been just such a one now. But she knew he loved her. He told her so, every day in that letter in the blue envelope. She knew also that he owned a great house in the English countryside (but lived in his London Club) as well as this flat in Paris which he insisted belonged to her. There had been papers for her to sign to that effect. She had not needed his protection, for her father had left her very well provided for. Her sister, who had married, and left France to live in Scotland, had a daughter who came to visit every year. She had watched Laura growing up, in beauty and independence; and loved her all the more, because she came, against her parents' wishes, and asked no questions. Someday Laura would meet Andrew, and hear the whole story and understand. She smiled to herself. Andrew had telephoned the night before, from his club in London, to say he would be coming for a long stay in Paris this time – his work transferred to the Elysees for at least four months. They had both fallen silent at the telephone, so deep was their delight, even after years of devotion, at the prospect of being together. Fabienne leaned over and looked at the photograph in a silver frame, on the table beside her bed. How handsome he was.

Their first meeting had been at Deauville, where her parents spent a month every summer. The long stretch of fine sands and cool breezes, the Casino where you could risk a few francs or a fortune – or perhaps watch an old-fashioned operetta in the little ornate theatre (the heroine was always blonde, dressed in pink, and singing flat, against a background of palms and spindle-legged chairs). Andrew had looked very British in his white flannels and cricket sweater, striding along the beach every morning. He always said that he had 'picked her up' and that she had responded eagerly. The result is what mattered. Introduced to her parents, Monsieur and Madame Larmontier, he had been asked to their house in the Loire valley, before he went back to England to start working for the government. Like all good French parents they had found out all about him – their eldest daughter had already been married off to a Scotsman, so they were used to the routine. It had been a glorious weekend, and before it was over, Andrew had given her a turquoise studded ring, and their faith in each other had been established. Then, darkness fell and the war swept over Europe: Fabienne and her parents moved to Paris. Andrew joined up at once in England; her father, in the 'reserves' as all middle-aged Frenchmen seemed to be, was called back into the Army, and her mother was matron in a military hospital. Fabienne, and her young idealistic friends grew restless and formed a group in the Resistance. She knew they would be survivors, Andrew and herself, and when, after months she had no censored words from him and he was reported 'missing', she gained strength and certainty. She often reviewed all this, now, and marvelled. They were growing old, without noticing it, she decided. And here was yet another spring morning, and Lili's knock at the door – and ah! the fragrant smell of that strong coffee!

'Come in. Any letters?'

'A few, Madame Fabienne. One from London.'

Lili always enjoyed watching her mistress tear open the envelope, as she poured out the coffee for her.

'He is coming next week, Lili – for a long stay this time. Miss Laura's visit will have to wait.'

She lay back on her pillows. How wonderful life was – every sight and sound of this spring day belonged to her, as Andrew had now, for well over twenty years. They had never felt they needed marriage or children. Their growing into each other's lives had been complete. She had visited him a few times in London, and had stayed at Claridges, but Paris was home to them both. Andrew had explained long ago that the great house in Wiltshire was a family heirloom, and meant nothing to him – all he said was: 'It is properly cared for. I never want to live in it, or see it again.' He spoke of his sister, but she had married and gone to Canada and settled there, and had no children. So Fabienne was the pivot of his life. She knew every corner of his mind, every inch of his body, every worry, delight, or idea that beset him, his digestion, and even the length of his toe-nails – all were her concern. She knew he hated linen sheets with embroidered borders, luke-warm baths, sweetbreads, and any shade of green. And he was just as aware of her. There is little to be said about happiness. The condition is indefinable, mysterious, insatiable, and as easily forgotten as pain. Now their four months together went by and Andrew returned to London; into a maze of governmental plot and plan, with hardly time to write his daily letters – as always, he was cloaked in the fulfilment of the weeks he had been with Fabienne. She was his matching self, his contentment, deepening year by year.

The colours of Paris were turning grey and murky. The lamps were lit at five o'clock and people hurried along without lingering on the benches in the Tuileries or Luxembourg Gardens. The smell of petrol took over from the flower-markets, and answers were curt at the kiosks. Winter was coming, and there was no escaping it. The glass enclosures went up at the cafés, and little fur pieces appeared on the coats of the girls walking the boulevards.

Two weeks after Andrew left, Fabienne welcomed Laura. The evenings growing darker, they played gin-rummy, Fabienne cheating, her glasses slipping down her nose. They watched the very shaky black and white television (colour was just creeping in), ladies with bee-hive hair-do's, sitting next to a high vase of plastic flowers, rattled out the news, dealing smugly only with France, occasionally stretched to Swiss borders. One day, in despair Laura bought the 'London Times', hoping to catch up with the world in general. Its appearance in Fabienne's flat caused upheaval and grief. On the editorial page, an article full of praise and regret, announced the sudden death of Andrew Forrestor, six days before. Laura saw Fabienne turn pale and tremble, and cry out for Lili, as she slumped in her chair in a dead faint. Lili, with tears pouring down her face, helped Laura to get Fabienne undressed and put to bed: the doctor was called and gave her a sedative, and left orders with Laura to call him the next morning. All Lili would say to Laura was:

'It is not my place, Miss Laura, to explain.'

The next morning Laura slept late. She dressed slowly, dreading what the day might hold and was astonished to find Fabienne, looking serene and beautiful, waiting for her at the table by the window, the Sèvres coffee pot at hand: there was a mist on the Seine, and the tops of the

rees below the balcony were turning to gold. They talked
of mundane things, and Laura asked no questions but was
feverish with curiosity. Fabienne turned away the
moment sympathy welled up in Laura's wide gaze.

'We will talk this evening. I am glad you are here,
Laura. We will take a long walk today – when the mist
clears. And now, telephone Dr Renault and thank him,
and say I am quite recovered. He knew Andrew very well,
you see, and must be sad.'

Lili came in with a tray, her face swollen after a sleepless
night, silent, looking very cross as she cleared away the
breakfast things. She fished in her apron pocket and
handed a long white envelope to Fabienne.

'This came.' And she hurried out of the room.

'I don't think I want to open it. Laura, perhaps you will
read it, and tell me what it says.' In the upper left-hand
corner, in fine engraving: 'Amberson and Amberson,
Solicitors'. The stamp was English, posted three days
before in London. Laura read the letter aloud in a pinched
voice:

'Dear Madame Larmontier: It was with great regret
that we learned of the death of our valued client, Andrew
Forrestor. We beg to inform you that he left with us a
letter, to be opened after his death, in which he advised us
to let you know that when his estate is auctioned (as he was
certain it would be, since there is no heir) he wishes you to
choose any object or objects in the Manour House that you
may want. He also asks you to let us know at the time what
day you wish to travel to London, and we are instructed to
attend to your ticket, also a ticket for anyone who
accompanies you, and we are to reserve hotel rooms in
London. The auction will take place on the sixteenth of
November and we will expect you to visit Forrestor House
the day before the sale, to inspect its contents. Please

confirm that you will arrive in London before November fifteenth. Faithfully yours, Amberson and Amberson.'

'So.' Fabienne took the letter from Laura, and held it unseeing. She looked out of the window. It amazed her to see life going on, as usual. Just as it had amazed her this morning, to see that she had a face, when she looked in the mirror; she felt skinned alive.

'Will you go with me, Laura?' she asked.

'Of course. I'll drive you down from London. My car is quite comfortable.'

'This must all be very mysterious to you. I knew Andrew before the war. We have been together since then. We are everything to each other. Were everything.'

'How dreadful for you, Aunt Fabienne. Dont' talk about it now. I know how unhappy you must be – and you'll only make yourself ill.'

'Unhappy? Nonsense. I had the most wonderful life; I'm so grateful. There never was anyone else. For either of us. Write to them and say we will be at Claridges on the fourteenth of November. And then you can drive me to Wiltshire in your little car. And now let me be alone for a while.'

How strange to know she would be alone for always. Even as she thought it, she heard Andrew's voice saying, as he always had when he thought he had displeased her – 'Forgive me; I didn't mean it.' It had been enough. At last, Fabienne allowed herself a healing flood of tears.

Within the week that followed, Laura had heard the whole story.

'Weren't you ever jealous?'

Fabienne laughed. 'Of what?'

'I mean – he spent so much time away from you. You said, a few years at the beginning.'

'Just waiting to come back. As I waited.'

'I don't think I could ever do that.'

'I know. Love today has to be so immediate. So much flavour is lost.' She smiled. 'Perfection takes time. Do you remember your first visit to me?'

'I was eleven. I'll never forget it!'

'What is the thing you remember most?'

'Ice-cream at Rumpelmeyers!'

'And I had to wait and wait, while you ate it very slowly. Each spoonful seemed to take an hour. "To make it last" you told me. Do you understand what I'm saying?'

'Darling Aunt Fabienne. I think I understand everything about you. I can't believe that was twenty years ago. And I remember a day when a tall man rushed in with some flowers for you, and out again before I could see him properly. Was that Andrew?'

'He was just going back to England for a week or so. He always remembered you standing there, with your mouth open and a bow in your hair, watching us. After that, I made sure you only came to see me while he was away. Your mother would have accused me of corrupting the young. You would have only learned how splendid love can be.'

'I envy you, Aunt Fabienne.'

There was a box on the floor, full of photographs. Fabienne's hands shook as she put them in order. Lili came in to light the fire. It was the end of October; the tickets to London and their passports, the hotel reservation, were all neatly ready in the desk drawer. Laura looked at them every day, with apprehension. She wished Fabienne would not go. There seemed no need, no reason.

London was teeming with a pre-Christmas festive activity, as usual in mid-November. The evenings were crisp, all shop windows alight; the silent excitement that somehow gathers in the early dusks of winter, and makes people hurry to wherever they are going – scuttling into the burrows of the underground to get home. (There is no other season when men so resemble moles and badgers.) Claridges was buzzing too, when Fabienne and Laura arrived there on November fourteenth: it was the hour of tea-assignations. In the pillared hall, the orchestra was accenting the pastel Edwardian atmosphere, weighted with marble and worn gilding, the chromatic violin sounds of Rimsky-Korsakov's 'Hymn to the Sun' piercing the chatter and clatter and laughter that was lost in the space and height of that famous trysting place.

Fabienne looked around delightedly, from behind a round table in a corner.

'It has not changed at all. China tea, please.'

Laura was not looking forward to the next day. They were going to start early, her car was in order in the garage, and she had traced her way carefully on the road-map. The solicitor had very kindly sent clear directions how to get to the Forrestor Estate, in Wiltshire, near Trowbridge. Fabienne leaned back in her brocaded arm-chair. There was always one at each tea-table. She half expected to see Andrew walk in, brief-case in hand, still with the cares of the day on his mind, his eyes searching to find her in the crowded lobby. The tea came, too hot to touch, with an assortment of cakes more like Mr Kipling's than a French pastry-cook's. It was all tinged with an imitation of past elegance, and a perfect frame for Fabienne. Laura would have relished a very dry Martini at that moment.

The next morning they drove silently along country lanes, the flowing patchwork of autumn colours against a leaden sky. Fabienne insisted on stopping for lunch at a village pub, where the locals stared hard at the two of them, Fabienne in her mink coat, drinking wine.

'The old one's French' the barmaid confided to one of her regulars, 'and the other one asked the way to the Forrestor place. The auction's there tomorrow. We'll have a crowd in, you can be sure.'

Laura was not prepared for the size of the park, its alley-ways of trees, its statues and fountains. There was even a Folly, hidden in a grove, reflected in a small lake, a small temple with moss and ivy clinging to its discoloured pillars. The large house at the end of the drive was austere, its windows like dead eyes; the great door open, where two men were directing the viewers. As yet, not many people. Laura said she would rather stay outside – wander in the grounds, and wait in the car. She felt chilled to the bone. She watched her aunt walk shakily on her high heels over the gravel, up to the door.

As Fabienne stepped over the threshold her heart sank. Everything was so huge here – the great double staircase, the paintings, the forbidding high-backed chairs against the walls. Everything over-sized, over-polished. Long tables with priceless silver and porcelain on view, dripping chandeliers, a library of seemingly a thousand books. She hesitated to walk on the silk Persian rugs, and did not dare to even go near the velvet ropes stretched across half a room, to keep some perfect French furniture away from the touch of human hands. A few people were reading catalogues and talking softly as they looked at the white price tags dangling from ormolu clocks and Chinese vases. Now and again, a grey-faced man in a dark blazer would warn someone apologetically not to touch, and then walk away, his hands clasped behind his back, his eyes still watchful. It was cold, it was heartless, depressing, and as Andrew had once said, it had nothing to do with him. Fabienne could find no hint of him anywhere. Surely, there must have been a childhood hidden away here, somewhere? So she braved the hallway, and climbed up the great staircase. There were people milling about, staring and appraising, mostly antique dealers, she thought, cruelly impersonal buyers. She opened a door along a wide corridor. The sun was coming into a casement window and slanted on an easeled black-board, dusty with old chalk. A desk, a rocking-horse; on the wall, a calendar procaliming the year 1924. A warmth stole over her. There was a photograph on the mantel-shelf. A school cricket team; and there, among the boys, a thin, fair Andrew. Unmistakeably Andrew.

A noise made her turn. The man in the blazer stood in the doorway.

'Sorry Madam, this is the private part of the house. Nothing in the sale, up here.'

Fabienne apologised, shivered, and wrapped her mink coat tightly around herself as the man led her downstairs. He ushered her into a warm room. It was obviously the portrait gallery. Family portraits, at least four centuries of them. A few people were peering at them. In uniform, in armour, in Judge's robes, even the scarlet of a Cardinal; and the women too, posed, immaculate; only one, in late nineteenth century costume, seemed vaguely familiar. It might be Andrew's grandmother, she thought. A shaft of sunlight warmed the wall by the marble fire-place, and she was drawn by it towards a small painting, in a deep gold frame, hiding under the great ones on the wall, almost excusing itself for being there. It was Andrew, painted by some modern unknown artist, just as she had known him before the war. His lean young face, deep-set eyes; a splash of blond hair – hurtingly alive, as the paint caught the sunlight. This was what she had come for. She did not know how long she stood there. She felt triumphant, exalted. She must have said his name aloud.

'You knew him?' A large woman in heavy tweeds was standing next to her.

She answered guardedly. 'Yes. Since before the war.'

'Oh?'

'It is so like him, isn't it? A wonderful portrait.'

'You are French – your accent?'

'From Paris. I am just over here for the auction.'

She must be careful, as careful now as she had always been for his career, his importance, his life. The big Englishwoman was looking at her strangely.

'Did you know him well – Madame . . . Madame?'

'Larmontier. Fabienne Larmontier. Yes, I knew him very well. And you?'

'I am his wife.'

Dr Stein

It was a pleasant Saturday afternoon in one of the well-kept green-belt estates. The songs of the lawn-mower, watering hose and rake were punctuated by a blackbird's mating call, molten Rock pouring from the radios and from somewhere (perhaps Mars) a Mahler symphony straining to be heard. Harold stopped mowing the grass, and leaned on the high handle of the machine. He wasn't feeling very well. All week, in the office, in his unspecified Civil Service assignments, he looked forward to these two days of rest and quiet, which he never got. It had been better when the children were still at home; they had done a lot of the things he was doing now, and he could exercise his authority – what was left of it.

The houses were set well apart, with pebbled drive-ways, and annexed garages – all different in style – red brick Georgian prevailing, with white doors and window-frames that had to be painted every two years. This year Harold had been startled by his own impulse to splash bright purple paint where white was decreed. (Of course he didn't.) He and Alice had lived here for twenty-five years. They had never had a quarrel (she announced this to anyone at any place, any time), their children had not worried them overmuch, and their holidays had been uncomplicated. They drank moderately, went into London once a month for shopping, and a theatre or concert. Their cultural life was not over-stocked. An ideal middle-class middle-life?

One upset, which lasted for two days. Strangely, about the painter, Paul Gauguin. They had seen a film, and read a book about him. Alice denounced his behaviour furiously – Harold upheld it. It had been their one disagreement. Harold viewed Alice's taste uncritically – taking it for granted that anything she chose would be the right colour, the right shape. He ate what she cooked with thankfulness and seeming pleasure. Their routine remained unruffled, their house neat, their bills paid. Their personal habits were considerate of each other; in other words, what was the matter? Some invisible treachery was at work. Harold felt ill; Alice made him go to the doctor, who could not find anything the matter with him. He went to specialists who found nothing out of order. 'A fine specimen' they all said. His work suffered, and he was called to the head-office, where they had a little talk with him, so that he came home depressed.

The following week Alice was having tea in the shop in the high-street where they sold 'home-made' cakes wrapped in cellophane and marked with a trade name. Stella, her special friend, met her there, and as usual, chattered away: the week's gossip, prices in the market, her husband Ned's bad temper, her children's punk hair-dos, and she finally said, putting down her cup:

'And how are you, Alice?' Alice, of course, had no news. Everything was going as smoothly as a skating-rink, provided you took care.

'And how is Harold?' Stella added.

'He's fine. The doctors say he's in splendid shape. It was a silly scare.'

'Men are funny at his age, you know.'

'What do you mean, Stella?'

'Well, they have change of life the way we do – but we usually don't bother about it. They do.'

'Nonsense.' Alice giggled a bit.

'It isn't nonsense. The best doctors admit it's true.'

'But surely nothing changes physically with them?'

'It does, you know.'

'How awful.'

'Don't be silly. It's just a natural progression. Getting older.'

Alice couldn't enjoy her tea. She felt terribly unsophisticated. Stella knew so much. She had explained circumcision, Yoga, lesbians, and the Foreign Market, when necessary. She always gave Alice the feeling of a new dimension: it took days for it to sink in, before it vanished without trace into the steady stream of her life. On principle, she would not read books that would tell her anything new, except cook-books and 'Do it Yourself' literature. But she was well-read in the minor classics and the Oxford Book of English Verse. It was enough in her busy life, she thought. Busy? Anyway, she retained a kind of mental purity – and certainly a physical one.

'I'll send you a book about it.'

'O, please don't, Stella. Harold might see it.'

Stella sighed. It was no use. Alice belonged to the great incorruptibles – she was a prize ninny, she thought, but couldn't help being fond of her.

'When will you both come to dinner? It's been weeks!'

'I'll let you know. I'll have to ask Harold. He doesn't seem to want to do anything.' Alice put on her scarf which made her look like a blonde Russian immigrant. Her shopping bag was overflowing, she kissed Stella, and went off on her bicycle. Half a mile down the high street, she turned left, and then down a hidden lane towards home.

The television gazed at her with a blind eye. She was never tempted to switch it on, unless Harold wanted to watch a nature film or snooker; they both abhorred the violent death-dealing news, and the absurd diamond and caviar veneer of American millionaire fiction; and they were equally uncomfortable watching that middle section, those serials which seemed like a peep-show into the life they recognised. Sometimes they admitted, they had seen something, or someone magnificent, and they were visibly nourished. Stella would know it, meeting Alice in the post-office the next morning – there would be a shine about her, as though she had taken a lover.

On this day, when Alice got home, she fed her welcoming cat, and decided to try a new recipe for Harold's dinner. She hoped he would be feeling better, this evening. Their marriage had been perfect, she thought, and since the children had gone away to their own lives, even more tranquil. Alice considered herself at the best time of life, forty-five (well, a bit more, really) but only a wing of greying hair to show it, which was most becoming, especially with her large hazel eyes, and fresh complexion. She believed that the older you got, the more careful you had to be – so Harold had never seen her with cold cream on her face, or a curler in her hair; she never left the bathroom door open, or allowed herself the sights and sounds of cosy intimacy. A pity. But then he was just as selfconscious and fastidious. Stella knew this, and sometimes behaved outrageously on purpose, trying to make them break the pattern. (She could make Harold laugh, anyway.)

By the time Harold came home, the kitchen could have been an illustration for House and Garden; the casserole was in the oven, the cheese-cake in the fridge, waiting its turn. His bath-towel on the hot rail, his clean shirt spread out on the bed. And Alice, in the garden, watering the petunias. He came up the path, umbrella, brief-case and evening paper properly in hand.

'I'm sorry I'm late,' he said, kissing Alice on the cheek.
'I'll have my shower and change. Gin and tonic, please.'
He walked past her and the hose, and disappeared into the
house. Alice finished the water, took off her gardening
gloves and went in after him. 'That was odd, he usually
drinks sherry' was her thought.

When Harold came into the living room, he looked
flushed and worried.

'What is it darling? What's happened?'

'I've had an awful day. Sort of black-out. Couldn't find
some important papers they needed. Then they found
they'd given them to someone else. No apologies. They
just don't believe anyone.'

'What do you mean, a blackout?'

'I just conked out. Found myself stretched out on the
black leather settee in the head-office. They were all very
concerned, but the doctor said it was nothing to worry
about. They've given me a week off. Doctor says it was
shock. Shock to myself – making a possible mistake, he
said. I can well believe it.'

'Poor darling. I can believe it too. Are you all right
now?'

'Right as rain. Don't give it another thought. This gin
tastes good. Better than sherry. Let's have another.'

Alice's eyebrows shot up, almost to her neat wavy
fringe. But she poured out his gin, without comment. She
was secretly very disturbed.

The week passed gently; it rained most of the time, so
Harold sat indoors reading, and when Alice was out at the
supermarket he would put on Radio 3, and hope for the
best. He helped with the dishes, and made their morning
tea, and their night-cap Ovaltine. Not exactly ebullient
at any time, he was withdrawn, and did not sing 'The
Road to Mandalay' in the bath, as usual. He refused to see

anyone, and Alice heard him swearing at the cat.

'We must talk about it, whatever it is,' she said to him one evening when he had refused her splendid pudding; and afterwards, when she told him that their married daughter had telephoned to say she was pregnant, all he said was 'Poor child'. Alice didn't know whether he meant his daughter, or the coming infant.

But Harold refused to talk. When the week was up, his work-routine started again, and no more was said. But he looked pale and drawn, and remained depressed.

During the coming week, Stella tried to help. Alice met her in the cake-shop for tea.

'Alice, if the doctors say there's nothing the matter with him, we'll have to start thinking about another kind of treatment.'

'He's quite all right.'

'He needs psychiatry, obviously.'

Alice gasped.

'You mean he's mentally ill?'

'No-no-no! But something's worrying him – something he doesn't even know about. Psycho-somatic, they call it. Almost everybody goes to an analyst now – in the States it's like going to the dentist, or having body-massage once a week. We've got to help him, and you must be sensible.'

'Harold would never agree,' Alice said.

'Well then, you must make him – use every wifely persuasion – I'll keep out of it, but Alice dear, you have got to make him see sense, for both your sakes.'

'But I don't know any psychiatrist.'

'I'll find out the best. And telephone you when I know. Come on, eat your cake now, and calm down. And stop asking Harold how he feels; that's the worst thing you can do.'

'O, dear.' Even a slight unhappiness gave Alice a great

136

appetite for sweets and Stella watched, amused and sad, while several pink-iced, cream filled cakes were forked away to the last crumb.

During the next week Alice brought up the subject of psycho-analysis. Harold looked at her, unbelieving, lost his temper, and went out for a walk. That was on Saturday. On Sunday she talked about it again, saying that if he really loved her he'd listen. So of course he did. After that she just waited. Then, one evening, he put down his newspaper and said: 'What's that fellow's name? The one you wanted me to see?'

Alice's heart lifted in joy, but she just said:

'Who are you talking about?'

'That analyst man. I've thought it over. I owe it to us both. And I feel so low, I'll try anything. You've been very patient with me.'

'His name is Dr Stein'. And she went over to where he sat in the big arm-chair, leaned down, and put her arms around him.

He pushed her away gently. 'Take it easy, Alice.'

She poured out two big gins and they clicked glasses. He said, with a kind of gentle mockery,

'Here's to Dr Stein. Our good angel.'

The next day Harold arranged for twelve one-hour weekly sessions of confession and cure. (Paid in advance.)

The summer ended. Harold grew rosy and cheerful again, and Alice wrote to Dr Stein to tell him how grateful she was. She got a typewritten answer, saying the absolute cure was not yet in sight, but that every session meant progress, and that by October the analysis should be complete. Her husband was a very interesting case. 'And so he should be' Alice thought, 'at fifty pounds an hour.'

Every Friday evening Harold came home an hour later than usual, as the weekly appointment with Dr Stein was

137

after his office hours. Alice never asked questions, but relished the return of her husband's good humour, almost jaunty walk, bursts of laughter – even if he seemed preoccupied. He would sometimes bring her flowers, and they had an outing to the Festival Hall for a concert (and those terrible sandwiches in the big foyer). The river looked beautiful, with thousands of lighted windows on the opposite bank vying with the starlit black sky. Alice tried to talk intelligently about the music, but knew she failed miserably. She watched Harold's face soften, and the muscles in his cheek work like a pulse, as the conductor and soloist came to the end of the Shostakovitch concerto – she was shut out of his world. Grateful, for all that, that she had been sitting beside his enjoyment.

'You see,' said Stella, when they met for coffee the next morning, 'everything will be wonderful again.'

'It's been terribly expensive,' Alice murmured, 'but of course that doesn't matter as long as Harold's well.'

'He's really himself again?'

'More than that,' Alice said. 'He's much more thoughtful. He remembered our anniversary. Twenty-six years – imagine! And he seems happy at the office too. Almost as though he was taking a new view of things – or had made up his mind about something.'

'Dr Stein is a very clever man. We'll have to have a dinner party the night of his last session. A sort of welcome back for him. When is it?' Stella asked.

'Two weeks more. You and Ned must come to us, of course. We'll have a real celebration. What fun!' Alice's eyes sparkled. She saw how it would be – she would buy two bottles of Heidsieck, and wear her black velvet. There would be the glow of candlelight, and the three of them welcoming him. Stella read her thoughts and cut across her dream:

138

'It's not another honeymoon, Alice – life goes on, you now. But I'm so glad I persuaded you. There's nothing like a good dose of analysis.'

And they went their ways in the supermarket.

t was the night of jubilation. Stella and her husband, Ned, were waiting with Alice. Everything was ready: yellow roses on the table, candles sputtering in their silver sconces, the velvet curtains drawn to shut out the damp October evening. Harold was already half an hour late. Alice asked Ned to open the champagne – an ice-bucket was ready to keep it chilled – and they sat, the bubbles going flat in the glasses, their ears straining to hear a key in the door; keeping up an imitiation of cheerful conversation, wondering, apprehensive.

A car stopped outside, and they heard Harold's voice say 'Wait please.' There was no time to solve that mystery, because suddenly he was there, in the doorway, strong, bright, assured. Before anyone could say a word, he looked straight at Alice, and spoke very clearly, without emotion, his voice full, his syllables precise:

'I've come to say goodbye. No – don't interrupt, please, Alice. I've found out what has been the matter, why I have been ill. I am going away; I've signed everything over to you – the house – the car – my account, and shares; the papers are all at the bank. I have always hated this house, and everything in it. I have hated our way of life – and after all this time Alice, I'm afraid I hate you. I am never coming back. Thanks to you, and Dr Stein. Forgive me if you can.'

All that could be heard was the sound of keys being dropped on the hall table, the front door closing softly, and the wheels of a car on the gravel as it drove away.

139

Portrait of Minnie

Somewhere, dug deep into the moorlands, there prospers the town of Blakely. A minor Cathedral, an out-of-date cotton-mill, a cinema and a superb eighteenth century theatre, lure the occasional tourists to explore, and they are well rewarded. For two months in summer, its narrow streets and market square are crowded with camera-hung visitors, pottery-shops and tea-rooms overflowing, its cathedral aisles alive with whisper and footsteps. On Armistice Day the whole town turns out to honour its dead heroes of two wars, with the local factory band in full blast and poppy wreaths piled beneath the granite obelisk with its names carved into the stone. Christmas too, with carol singers, and a big tree in the square – and the pantomime. Every year a pantomime comes for a six week season – usually a number two or three touring company, because it is possible that the London moguls have never heard of Blakeley and its theatre, grandly called 'the Queen Victoria'.

It is a dream of a theatre. Two tiers of boxes held up by slender white columns to a steep gallery, with carvings of gilded cherubs and a painted ceiling of the muses on billowing clouds. There is dark red damask on the walls, a mahogany bar, and dark, dusty passages leading to 'back-stage', that secret kingdom since the beginning of theatre time. When the faded velvet curtains swing open and closed, there is a gust of star-dust, a tinsel sprinkle; then a hush, and if you have the mind to, you can hear faint laughter – and perhaps the boom of a sonorous voice belabouring verse, and fading into nothingness.

Up three flights of stone stairs, behind the stage, there is a room where Minnie Robbins, her needles and thread, her kettle and her ironing-board are the heart of the matter. She has been there more years than she cares to say. She has much more work to do now, because no company travels 'dressers' as they used to do; so it is she who takes care of every costume as it comes in, and attends to the zipping up and quick changes of the leading ladies and gentlemen – it is quite a rest at pantomime time, because it means six weeks of the same company. Sometimes it is even the same players who come year after year, and they call her pet names, and treat her to a gin or two, and even a pound note now and then if she does any laundry for them. She sits, dreaming, sewing on spangles and mending the 'Aladdin' costumes most of the Christmas holiday, a heavy woollen shawl pulled tight across her shoulders, because the weather-soiled window lets in the draught, and even a lost snowflake or two. She smiles to herself, and sings along with the horns and flutes and violins that are practising in every available corner – even on the staircase landing outside her door.

Stella Robbins had a lover; his name was Sidney Warrington, and he kept her swathed in furs and ringed in diamonds; he also bought her a theatre and lost a fortune putting on plays for her whenever she felt a longing for display. She was not a good actress, but the public grew to love her face and the aura of romance that trailed her like perfume. When she suddenly announced her retirement, and then the birth of her child, there were a few items in the newspapers, and then oblivion. But she remained in the shadow of the theatre, and after Mr Warrington deserted her, took any job that was offered to provide for er daughter, Miranda, who was taken along with the trunks and hampers, as Stella traipsed up and down the country with a touring company, in that uncertain peace between two wars. Stella was wearing out, along with the furs and finery Mr Warrington had provided (the diamonds had been sold long ago); and Miranda was growing prettier and talented enough to command attention.

One cold Christmas week, when poor, tired Stella succumbed to pneumonia and died, it was a foregone conclusion that Miranda, just turned twenty, would become a useful player in the company, after she had learned to live with her grief. It took her three years to get to London and a small role in what James Agate called an unimportant comedy'. But one night the fairy-tale evolved. The star of the play fell ill, and Miranda, who was her understudy, triumphed. All the trimmings of success didn't matter very much to her, because she was in love with an actor in the Company who had comforted and encouraged her. Bill Jamieson was a handsome young man, patterning himself on old photographs of Owen Nares and Ronald Coleman. He called her Minnie and taught her all he knew about the theatre (and everything else), both of them taking it for granted that one day, when they had time, they would get married.

That September, the lights went out. Minnie had hardly been aware of the possibility of war, so protected and snug in her theatrical cocoon; and when the theatres closed, and Bill was called up, she went into a dark trance for days. Nothing was real any more, except the wail of the air-raid siren. She followed crowds into shelters without question, and felt like a manipulated thing – without blood or will. When Bill came to say goodbye in a uniform that seemed to be made of brown blotting paper, they managed to play their final scene beautifully. She had his

143

photograph in uniform, framed in curly brass, and kept ｉ
beside her bed. For a while letters came, and then sudden
ly stopped. Minnie was working in munitions, by tha
time, where the girls in their bright head-scarves had grow
shells as hard as the ones they polished for mass murder

One day she read that ENSA wanted 'ladies who coul
dance and sing, to go abroad to entertain the fightin
forces'. She tore off her knotted head-scarf and rubbe
gloves, and rushed back to her cubicle at the YWCA t
manicure her nails and wash her hair, and find her way t
Drury Lane.

The elderly stage-manager looked bemused when sh
gave her name.

'Robbins? Robbins? I remember a Stella Robbins whe
I was a lad in the Midlands. Any relation?'

'She was my mother.'

'Well, well! Can you dance? Can you sing?'

'I can do both.'

'Good. Go over there and tell the pianist what musi
you want, and just sit there until we call you.'

Every girl who performed while she waited seemed t
her to have a stronger voice and better legs, but such wa
the need to fill the ENSA ranks that Minnie was signed on
and called for rehearsal. She was also told to be measure
for a uniform, and to be sure her passport was in order
and then she was handed over to a nurse in a white overall
who was waiting in the wings to inoculate the lucky girl
against diseases that bred in the war zones.

All that she remembered of those many months wer
the hundreds of eager faces, and khaki crowds under
blazing sun where bursts of distant fire in the sky vied wit
the orange and red of sand and blood. Most of the girl
found relief in drink and sex, in short supply – Minni
found it easy to reject both. As for the immediacy o

lovemaking, she only had to say that she had a fiancé somewhere near, and the balloon was pricked. She knew that it was because the over-heated soldiers respected her invisible lover, not the fact that she preferred to remain untouched. As she pranced on rickety platforms, she searched the upturned faces, day after day, wondering if she would ever see Bill's again, his eyes round with joyful surprise. By the end of the war she had seen most of the western world as far as the Arctic Circle.

In the spring of 1945 the concert party was sent to Iceland, where the Air Force were building a landing field. She was excited by the bleak hills of rock and ice – at any moment she felt they might rise up like monster dinosaurs to shake the earth under her feet, to destroy the greenhouses built over hot springs, where, in divine contradiction, flesh-coloured exotic plants and orchids flourished. The mysterious lunar atmosphere seemed a fitting climactic ending to months of a life totally disconnected with reality. After a few days the company was crammed into a heavily camouflaged army plane, which trembled in its blind flight like a tired moth. Hours later it ejected the ENSA-ites into an unrelieved blackness, somewhere in Britain.

Nothing seemed to matter any more. Minnie was more worried by the end of the war than she had been at its beginning and she suffered the inevitable de-mobbing ailment, feeling cast out and forsaken. She thought a lot about those last weeks in Blakely. Her mother holding her hand so tightly: 'Remember, darling, the only thing you know about is the theatre . . .'

She haunted the agencies for weeks. The answer was always nothing, nothing, and again nothing. After each dismissal she ached all over, as if she had been beaten, but rejection activated her resilient spirit.

145

It was that spirit that made her spend her last shillings for the journey to Blakely. When she arrived, it was a frosty morning, sun through crystal, and the slate of her mind was wiped clean. She got out of the train, and walked in the crunching snow, to the Queen Victoria Theatre. It was exactly as she remembered it. She knew what she was looking for – it was a door marked 'H. MILLBECK, MANAGER' at the top of some stairs with a fading carpet worn away in the middle of each step. She put down her suitcase outside the door, and knocked.

She was in luck. The pale man behind the desk listened with interest to her story, then went to an inner door and shouted for tea to be brought. A dusty adolescent with red hair came in with two mugs on a tray.

'This is Alfred, our call-boy now. He hopes to be an actor one day. This is Miss Robbins, Alfie, the daughter of Stella Robbins. You've seen her name on the posters in the bar.'

Alfie rubbed his hand on his jacket and offered a red paw.

'Gosh – think of that!' he said, 'shall I get you some biscuits?'

'No thank you. This tea is fine.'

As she sipped her tea, H. Millbeck was trying to think what he could do about her. She had told him she would do anything.

'We have more or less a permanent company' he said 'except for the pantomime at Christmas.'

'Of course.'

'Can you sew?'

'As well as most women, I think.'

'I hate to suggest this – but we do need somebody to take charge of the work-room: keep the costumes in order and even be a "dresser" when necessary. I'll understand if you refuse – but there's nothing else.'

'Mr Millbeck, you can't imagine how grateful I am. It's like coming home.'

146

It was all arranged. Alfie's mother had a room for her – and before a month was out, Minnie had it all her own way. Any theatre crisis was the breath of life to her, the stage-manager relied on her, the actors used her shamelessly, whether it was to mend a costume, hear their lines, buy a bottle of gin, or wash their shirts. She was happy. On some Sundays she would go to the churchyard to clear the weeds away from her mother's grave, and leave flowers.

The years passed very quickly and Minnie was growing old. The year she turned sixty, the company gave her a party, and a new sewing-machine. Mr Millbeck walked with two sticks now, and had grown a patriarchal beard, and Alfie had become the stage-doorkeeper because tannoys had been added to the new theatre equipment, and no call-boy was needed. His boyhood was long past, his mother dead, and Minnie had taken charge of his house for him.

That year the pantomime was 'Cinderella' – a very superior company was promised, with 'three West End stars'. Minnie cleared out the work-room and had more wall-hooks put up, and saw to it that the dressing rooms had clean curtains, new light-bulbs and no cracked mirrors. On December twenty-second the 'Cinderella' company arrived. Alfie bought the cast-list up to Minnie, and pinned it on her wall. She was very busy that day, and didn't look at it till late in the afternoon, when she put the kettle on. It didn't matter to her who was in it. Her glasses low on her nose, she ran her forefinger down the list of names. Her heart missed a beat, and panic seized her.

'The Baron . . . William Jamieson.'

Alfie found her sitting in the dark. She had made up her mind not to say a word about it.

Dress rehearsal was the next day. Minnie saw to it that all the costumes were in the right dressing rooms. But she kept the Baron's brocaded and embroidered coat and ruffles to deliver to him herself. She had spent half the night wondering how she would welcome Bill – or whether to welcome him at all. She had lost the habit of theatre-effusiveness – she decided on silence. The youthful image of Bill persisted. 'But he's older than I am' she kept telling herself. When the half-hour was called, roaring through the tannoy, she took the Baron's costume to his dressing room. A gruff voice answered her knock, and then a shouted obscenity.

'Where the hell have you been? What kind of a theatre is this – I want my costume in this dressing room every night before I get there. These bloody provincial theatres! And I want a bottle of whisky brought to me – now. Let me see that costume – they were supposed to let out the seams and there were two buttons missing –' he snatched the embroidered plum coloured coat from Minnie's arm, and turned it over. As he got up to try it on, he reeled a bit, and laughed. 'Don't worry, old lady. I've never missed a performance.'

He preened himself in his sweaty vest, in front of the long mirror, threw back his shoulders, patted his paunch and ran a hand over his balding dome, before he put on the beautiful coat. It fitted well. Minnie looked at his face in the mirror. Bloated, and blotched, with the wet lips parted in a grin to show his side-teeth missing, and pale, red-rimmed eyes above dark pouches, showing no flicker of recognition. She adjusted the white lace ruffles, and for a moment he stood still, erect, head held high, in an actor's stance, poised on the edge of magic mixed with alcohol.

Somehow she got out of the dressing room and stumbled up two flights of stairs into her work room, and stood, almost breathless, her back against the door, her eyes closed. He hadn't recognised her.

'Thank God,' she breathed. 'O thank God.'

148

Traveller's Return

The Honourable Charlotte Headley had lost hope. She knew her parents were waiting for her to marry and save them, and the dilapidated Victorian house in Belgravia from social and financial ruin. The only proposals she had had were from well-born dancing partners, unable to support a wife, let alone her parents. Fortunately she had not felt a spark of affection for any of them. It had been three years now since she had been dubbed one of the leading debutantes, and her petals were drooping. She was not exactly pretty, but had lovely dark hair, intelligent grey eyes, and a humorous sensitive mouth. Her childhood had been a delightful one, until she was sent off to Roedean, where the girls teased her and called her 'Apple-Charlotte' and 'Charlotte-Russe', so that she grew to hate her name. She had been called after an Aunt, who was supposed to have money; but when she died, she left nothing at all except a very old Cocker Spaniel, which her father had put down immediately. Edward Headley had tried hard, but had no business acumen, and was not helped by his inherited title or his unambitious, nervous wife. Roedean and several 'seasons' for Charlotte had left him with nothing except a deep wish to retire to a bungalow near Bournemouth where he would breathe deeply of relief and sea-air. Charlotte sensed all this, and because she loved her parents, she was unhappy. She had done all the right things, and knew all the right people. Good manners, she had been taught, were the sweetness of life, if not the spice. Minor discomforts were to be endured, and she must never argue with the servants. Since no servants were available, there must be no complaints, and there must never be a mention of the need for anything money could buy. It wasn't a question of being better than anyone – she just knew where she belonged, even if her world no longer existed.

Then she met Sam Pickering, a newly-minted tycoon from the North; self-made, honest, seeking a softening well-bred file for his rough edges; his eyes lit upon her at a garden-party and he decided he wanted her. He had a great deal to offer; a large house in the wide countryside near Manchester, an army of amicable servants, three outsize cars; rooms always ready for him at the Savoy in London, and of course, himself. Rosy and rotund, with a burring North country accent, a balding head, and an undisguised ego, childishly optimistic. He had never been in love, he was much too busy. His sex-life had been tidy, reduced to rapid weekends, impersonal, uncommitted. He found in the Honourable Charlotte Headley the dream he had always dreamed. She would usher him into the magical world of well-bred protocol. And for her, it would be the end of worry. What she did not realise was that in the days and nights they would spend together, there would be a constant irritation, despite his kindness, an embarrassment, a tortuous insult to her senses, her tastes, her habits. And he was such a good man. The first thing he had done for her was to buy that longed for bungalow by the sea for her parents. They kept telling her how lucky she was.

She danced away the nights, trying not to mind Sam treading on her toes and ruining her silver slippers; and her friends admiring the huge diamond that labelled her as Sam's exclusive property. He laughed at her impatient criticisms, and at her fury when he called her 'the little woman' or, when they were alone playfully patted her small buttocks and called her 'Lottie'. Her rages made him even more loving. After they were married, he would grin at her down the length of their polished dining table, surrounded by guests, and tell the story of his poverty-stricken childhood in a mill town, his ailing mother, his father working in the mill and then killed in the war; over and over again. She learned to smile through it. As she did when he marched into restaurants ahead of her, and eyes twinkling, tucked his napkin into the top-button of his waistcoat, and told the waiter who handed him the wine-card to bring a carafe of 'red plonk'. He was always so good-humouredly amused at her discomfiture, and would change the order to 'the best bubbly' which did not help at all.

It had been one of the weddings of the year. Four years ago to the day. Charlotte looked at the rain slashing down against the window-pane and shivered in the Mancunian autumn. The night before for an anniversary present Sam had given her the ugliest piece of jewellery she had ever seen. A monster necklace of blazing multi-coloured gems, in a red velvet case, and his smile had been so loving that she had overdone her gratitude and invited him into the comfort of her bed. He had come into her room, happy, timid in his most expensive silk maroon striped pyjamas. She would never forget them. Towards morning when he left her, to sleep in his own bed in his dressing room next to hers, she lay awake wondering how she could get away, just for a while, without hurting him. She had not made friends in the North, and when she had invited Emma, her school-friend and bridesmaid, for a weekend, it was near disaster.

'Darling, how can you bear it? I know all about rough diamonds – but . . .' Charlotte laughed.

'You mean this is more like a craggy rock?' Emma forged ahead:

'He calls everyone "Luv" – even the housemaid.'

'Everyone who works for him adores him.' Charlotte found herself wanting to defend Sam as a tiger mother might her cub.

'And those terrible jokes! Absolutely schoolboy.'

'He's a marvellous husband. He spoils me.'

'He calls you "Lottie"!'

'At school you called me "Apple-Charlotte". Remember?' Emma's eyebrows shot up, and Charlotte fought through the weekend nobly.

It was spring when Sam agreed that Charlotte should go on a cruise in the Mediterranean. He reserved the best suite on board, and gave special orders to the Captain, and a large tip to the purser to care for 'my better half', and to make her voyage memorable. (This was quite unnecessary, as she would have the time of her life.) Sam came South with her to see her off. He hugged her and said 'I'll miss you', so seriously, in a voice gruff with emotion, that she felt guilty for an hour afterwards. She watched his chubby figure stride down the gang-plank, and she waved as the gleaming ship slid away into warm calm seas.

The first evening, she ordered dinner in her cabin. The square window looked out onto a slice of deck exclusively her own, a sun-chair spreadeagled, ready for tomorrow. She slept that night in a limbo that is only possible in trains and aeroplanes and ships at sea – out of contact, blissfully disorientated; and she woke late the next day feeling like a hopeful adolescent, her background receding. She dressed without much thought and forgot to make up her face, the freedom of anonymity suffusing her with joy.

On the upper deck she squinted into the sun – a strong wind was blowing and she tied a scarf over her hair, and under her chin. She might have been anyone, anywhere. There is nothing that breaks barriers more crisply: Mrs Jones in the supermarket, or Her Majesty looking at horses on a dull day, the head-scarf is the symbol of sisters-under-the-skin. The sea was green and ruffled, lace-edged in a foam against the white paint of the ship's flanks, blinding in the sunlight. A tall, thin man, with a distinguished profile, and wearing a heavy grey pullover, came and leant out on the rail beside her.

'Splendid, isn't it?' A quiet cultured voice. He turned towards her. She looked straight into a stranger's eyes, and the voyage was chartered.

'Yes. Good after all the rain at home.' The man laughed. A nice, comfortable laugh.

'The weather is always an introduction isn't it? My name is George Fernshaw. And yours?'

'Charlotte Pickering.'

How was she to know that Mr Fernshaw had read the passenger list, questioned the purser and made up his mind. He was used to cruises, at least once a year, and always picked his companion carefully. At dinner, they found themselves at the Captain's table. George Fernshaw drew out her chair, asked her if she needed a shawl, and insisted, even if it was out of the order of things, that she was served first. (After the Captain, of course). The steward seemed pleased to obey, and the Captain was smiling, complaisant, his horizon blue eyes looking into distances beyond the passengers, while he ate whatever was put before him. Immaculate, gold-braided, his thoughts only focussed on the day or night ahead; in impersonal pre-occupation he managed to remember names somehow. The others at the table were an elderly couple celebrating their silver wedding, the headmistress of a girls' school and a young man of indeterminate nationality who never spoke unless spoken to. After a few days at sea Charlotte only had to suggest a vague wish – a piece of music she would like to hear; or a special dish for dinner and George made sure that it was granted.

She had never been showered with so many compliments or treated with such extravagant consideration. She told herself that this, this, was what she had always wanted. For the first time in many years she felt back in her own world. It was almost too much. She was trapped into utter femininity. Flowers filled her cabin after each port was touched upon, and if she admired anything on shore, it was there, beautifully packaged, waiting for her when she returned to the ship. The thought of Sam struck her like a gong several times a day. She was very much married, she reminded herself. It didn't seem to bother George however, and there was, so far, nothing that suggested seduction. Only the thoughts that buzzed in her mind like a mosquito.

They did not go ashore at Gibraltar, but leaned over the rail, side by side, in the sunshine, and watched the happenings. That morning, the ship's complement had exploded into 'whites' – to celebrate Southern waters, like a blaze of trumpets, and a great flash of light. Laughter and excitement and loud Latin voices drowned all British reserve in a hot turquoise sea. Charlotte was enchanted.

It was at Marseilles that she tried to find out more about George. They were having coffee at a bistro. She looked at him over the rim of her cup. His face looked chiselled out of flushed quartz, the expression kindly, amused. His eyes never quite met hers – or if they did, glanced away quickly. There was a faint hint of superiority – a rather haughty expression on his thin face. 'Breeding' Charlotte thought. She was very curious.

'How old are you?'

'Fifty-two. Twenty years ahead of you I'm sure. Does it matter?'

'What do you do?'

'Do?'

'Work. Profession – whatever? Let me guess. Something in the city? London I mean?'

'I don't live in London.'

'A country gentleman then?'

'You might call it that.' He laughed. 'You are way off the mark. Shall we leave it? I like being unlabelled. Don't worry. There's nothing sinister about me, I promise. Let's enjoy ourselves.'

They spent the day at Cassis, near Marseilles, where the rocks are red, and brave swimmers dive into eighty feet of indigo Mediterranean from the hotel garden by the sea. Charlotte's heart almost missed a beat watching these feats of bravado, while she enjoyed the Mephistophelean bouillabiase – all lobster claws, tentacles of octopus and spiky sea urchins. George chose a wine with a three-pronged name from a great tome in scarlet suede covers. In a corner of her brain she heard Sam's voice saying:

'Bring us a carafe of red plonk.' And found herself smiling.

'You're lovely when you smile.' So she beamed at him.

Later that evening back on board, she felt ill. Her eye-lids swelled up; garlic and shellfish did that to her, she should have remembered. She stayed in her cabin and drank a quart of Perrier Water, put Elizabeth Arden pads on her eyes and bolted the louvred door. She felt unaccountably depressed, devitalized, unchallenged. She did not know that it was Sam's abrasiveness she missed,

the way he had of debunking her, his clumsiness, his
no-nonsense lovemaking. She didn't realise, that it was
Sam who gave her something to battle against. Her
independence was nourished by his behaviour. What she
found lacking in him, gave her self-assurance, kept her
fighting fit. Now she felt soft, vulnerable, her surface
wishes all fulfilled. She went to bed and drew the covers
over her head to shut out the dance music coming from
somewhere amidships. It took three days for her to look
normal and feel well again. The purser had brought her
books, the doctor had visited her to be sure she wasn't
contagious, and hardly an hour passed, that a stewardess
did not bring her a message, a basket of fruit or something
that George thought might cheer her. When she finally
emerged unswollen, he was even more attentive than
before. At Cannes, the last stop on the cruise, he helped
her tenderly into the motorboat to take them to the
Marina. In twelve hours the passengers who now piled
into the launch would be on their way home, amazed at the
things they had bought: sun-hats and florid shirts they
would never need or wear, souvenirs that would find no
place in Aunt Dora's flat in Birmingham, toys that none of
their children would look at, and bunches of carnations
already wilting in the cabin washbasins.

Charlotte spent hours watching George win at roulette.
The Casino was empty in the afternoons and the croupier
resentful until George gave him a percentage of his
winnings with a quiet smile. There was an hour before
sailing and he ushered Charlotte into a jewellers where he
spent all his winnings on an exquisite gold and diamond
bracelet – narrow, perfect, discreetly designed. Of course
Charlotte refused it. But he was so clever, so logical in his
reasoning, that she found herself waltzing away the last
evening on board with it clasped on her wrist, draped over

156

he shoulder of George's white dinner jacket, where it sparkled in quiet beauty in tune to the waltz music and her heightened pulse beat. As the drums rolled a finishing chord, she had a sudden vision of a jewelled necklace hidden in her dressing table drawer at home – in its red velvet box, waiting.

On the last evening George tried to make love to her in a cinematic sort of way. He gave her a lingering, tight-lipped kiss in the best romantic tradition. She gave what she hoped was a Garbo smile, and moved three feet away. She felt she was acting in the end of an old film, black and white in the moonlight, with music throbbing in the distance. She said:

'I wonder if we'll ever see each other again?' She felt him stall, like a backing horse.

'Let's keep it a lovely interlude; a delightful mystery, something to remember always. I don't want to know anything more about you . . . it's been so perfect.'

'Have I been as dull as that,' she thought. George kissed her hand, and she trailed back to her cabin, to pack her suitcases. She put the bracelet into its slim white case, with a nice note to be left with the purser in the morning, and sighed a sigh of contented orderliness as she climbed into her narrow bed. It was two o'clock. There was a soft knock at the door, and before she could answer, George stood on the threshold in a dark dressing gown, holding a bottle of champagne and two glasses. He put them on the table.

'A last celebration,' he said, closing the door.

'I don't think so – please go, it's so late.' (Charlotte thought, so, the film isn't finished.) Out loud she said: 'I was going to leave this with the purser, but you can take it now,' and she gave him the bracelet in its case, and her letter.

'I shall throw it into the sea. I refuse to take it back. You know how I feel about you.' He smiled at her as he uncorked the champagne and it responded with a purr instead of a vulgar pop. He poured it into the glasses brought one over to her and sat on the bed at her feet What could she do, but drink it? She must contrive to look as though it meant nothing to her that a handsome man was sitting on her bed at two in the morning; he was behaving as she thought he might, and hoped he would not But it was worse than that. He was taking off his brocaded dressing gown. What happened next made her believe in providence, in the protection of the saints. He stood there in maroon-striped silk pyjamas. She started to laugh, and tried her best not to, but the dismay on his face was too much for her, and she burst into uncontrolled mirth. Sam in the same maroon stripes had looked like a shy clown Sam, Sam, dear timid, kind Sam. And those pyjamas! (He had been told by the best outfitters that they were what the sophisticated male must wear.) Sam! And here was George, leaving her cabin like an outraged Casanova, the bracelet in his pocket, closing the door carefully. She had said 'I'm sorry' but he had not the inner grace, poor man, to laugh at himself. She was delighted he had left the champagne, and drank another glass before she fell asleep.

It was foggy in Southampton. The passengers were leaving the ship, looking depressed. Charlotte went to the Purser's office.

'I'm sorry, but I forgot to ask Mr Fernshaw for his address. I want to write to him to thank him for all his kindness on the cruise.' The purser seemed to think this a most natural request.

'Ah, yes,' he said, looking in a large black book. 'The cabin was reserved by Lord Claybourne of Tavernleigh Park, Wiltshire.'

'Thank you.' But of course. Lord Claybourne would travel incognito. She knew of the Tavernleigh Estate – everyone did. And she remembered seeing pictures of his son's twenty-first birthday party in a glossy magazine. No wonder he wouldn't tell her about himself.

She decided to stay in London for the afternoon before going back to Manchester. She telephoned Sam from the Savoy, and said she wanted to do some shopping before coming north. He could not hide the happiness in his voice.

'As long as you're back, that's all that matters. Let me know what train tomorrow.'

She telephoned Emma and asked her to come and see her that evening. She felt she had to rid herself of her adventures before she saw Sam again. Emma had never betrayed her. Emma took life lightly, skippingly, and would ease her conscience. Towards sunset she looked out of the window and saw the lights strung out on the South Bank like decorations of a midsummer Christmas: and she felt the secret magic, the endurance, the everlastingness of London – she had not felt like that since she waved a flag at a Last Night of the Proms, years ago.

'Well,' said Emma, 'you look as though you've enjoyed yourself.'

'I have – in a way. I'm glad to be back.'

'Anyone exciting on the cruise?' Her eyes were looking steadily at Charlotte.

'There was this man . . .'

'There usually is – tell me more.'

'Nothing much to tell really – he just made me feel somehow back in my element – like some stranded fish suddenly popped back into its own little pool. He was the perfect escort – handsome, attentive – he seemed to know about everything. I know it sounds awful but he was the

159

very opposite of Sam – I felt guilty all the time for comparing them.'

'Why guilty? For the first time in years you've been able to be "the real you" – no wonder you enjoyed yourself.'

'The real me? I wonder? I'm not sure I know who that is any more. Anyway, that's enough about me – tell me your news.'

'Well,' Emma enthused, 'I'm about to have my own bit of cossetting at Tavernleigh next weekend. John Claybourne's asked us down – do you know him?'

Charlotte hoped her face was not as pale as it felt.

'I – I met him once – I thought him very attractive.'

'John! Attractive? – darling you can't be serious! But Tavernleigh's beautiful and such a wonderful place to stay. They have this incredible 'Jeeves' character who runs everything to perfection. One feels totally relaxed and luxurious; every whim catered for. I think John would have lost him years ago if he hadn't discovered his secret passion for foreign travel. He makes sure of keeping him by sending him off on some exotic voyage, first class, every year – all expenses paid! I'd give anything to see "our Jeeves" living it up on board. I bet he shoots a terrific line . . .' Emma chattered on, but Charlotte had disappeared into the bathroom.

Later that evening there was another telephone call to Manchester.

'Sam?'

'Lottie?'

'I'm coming home luv . . . the earliest train.'

The Silver Egg

His eyes were blue. Not the horizon blue of the sailor, or the misted searching blue of the airman. His were the burning zircon of a cat. When he first looked at her, she thought of madness, but discovered only mildness in his speech. They worked for the same publication – he wrote book reviews, and she visited luxurious houses, to find out when and why they were lived in; both their efforts appeared in print in the same glossy monthly magazine. They had been under the same working roof, passing each other in hall-ways, crushed close in soaring lifts, eaten sodden lunches in the canteen, sat across from each other at crowded board-meetings, and both of them had never, never ceased to wonder when or why they would finally get together. Here they were, at last; a Monday morning, waiting to see the Editor. The outer sanctum walls were of plate glass shrouded in huge greenery which seemed to grow as one watched, like the monster-plants in terror-television. In fact a vague terror was in the air; its name was redundancy. It had been fanning the offices for weeks.

They looked at each other and laughed.

'I'm Penelope Graham,' she said, 'it's absurd that we've never talked to each other before, isn't it? I know you're John Garner. I read your book reviews religiously.'

'I'm afraid I don't read your articles – but I know you are regarded with awesome respect by the drones. Hello, anyway – and about time too!'

'Do you know what we're here for?'

'I suspect they are getting rid of me.'

'I'm sorry.'

'I'm not!' His eyes were fixed on her face. She hated herself for blushing. She had been watching him for weeks, knowing he was unlike anyone in this enclosed world of magazine patter and chatter. She could start to be herself, she felt, even in this first exchange of words. She was not sure any more what that self was; even her name was not her real one – and she had exiled herself long since from a splendid house on the Borders. Already in her thirties, divorced and widowed, a career established, she had concentrated on work, assuring herself she needed no-one. She had pretended too long to belong to word-worn pages – some of them were in her hand now, ready to be approved by the Editor.

'What will you do if you leave here?'

'You must say "when" I leave. I shall go back to writing books instead of reading them. Don't look so surprised: I wrote three novels some years ago. Quite acceptable ones – one was made into a film, and it remains a cherished nest-egg in my bank. So don't be sorry for me.'

'I couldn't possibly be that.'

A blank-faced secretary appeared and said, 'Mr Garner please.'

He untangled his long frame from the plastic and chrome chair, straightened his shoulders and grinned at Penelope. She fell in love with him there and then. Fell, with a mighty thud, heart pounding, curiosity alerted, and the awareness of that chemistry of mind and body that warns of no escape. A few minutes later, he came out of the inner office, smiling:

'I'm a free man. Congratulate me.'

'O, I do, if it's what you want.'

162

'Celebrate with me. Have dinner?' Cautionary habit made her say –

'I – I – don't know if I can . . .'

'Nonsense. I'll meet you at Wheeler's. This is a scarlet-letter evening, after a red-letter day. Please come. I've no-one else to share it with, and you know you want to. Please.'

There was no use pretending any more. They had to start somewhere. She was totally unarmed against any attack on her sleeping sexuality, her unadmitted hunger. She realised this with delight, as she stepped over the threshold of the restaurant, and saw John waiting for her at a table in a quiet corner. It was a dream performance. Even to the rose lampshade, the glistening ice-bucket, the old waiter in a dusty black tail-coat. She thought, 'This could be anywhere in the world, and I am lost.' A package was by her plate.

'What's this?'

'A book I wrote ten years ago, when I was full of optimistic ego.'

'Which you are not, now?'

'Indeed not. All that has been washed away in the levelling flood of our magazine emporium. I shall gather momentum again, presently. I feel it coiling in me like a rusty spring. I don't mean the seasonal one – but I feel that, too.'

Penelope laughed. She fumbled with the string – he leaned across and pulled an end, and the parcel opened.

'I make terrible knots – secret ones that only I can untie.'

'I shall remember. Thank you for the book. I'll read it over the weekend.'

'It's only Monday. What did the editor want you for this morning?' John asked.

163

'To do more work.'

'A promotion?'

'I suppose you could call it that. I haven't decided what to do about it.'

The waiter appeared with cups of hot turtle soup. John said:

'I thought we'd have something hot, before the cold lobster. Why are you wearing a wedding-ring?' The question was sharply catapulted. She did not answer, and he leaned towards her, taut and insistent.

'Well? Are you married?'

'I was. Years ago. He went away with someone. I divorced him. He's dead now.'

'Then why are you acting ashamed?'

'I'm not ashamed, just not used to talking about myself.'

'And not used to being attacked by an inquisitive blunderer. Forgive me – but I want to know everything about you. And don't look at me like that – eat your soup, or do you belong to the faction that drinks soup?'

'It depends what kind of soup it is.'

Then it was John who never stopped talking – looking at her for comments of surprise or approval, which she gave, on cue. She was ready to accept him, no matter what. It was a rather bleak story, of an asthmatic childhood, a mother who had been a religious fanatic, a father who had vanished to Australia; a scholarship, and two years at Oxford; then the writing of books. No money, of course.

'So I took a job – looking after an estate belonging to the family of one of my Oxford friends – Maurice Taylor. It was in a warm climate, which I needed – with plenty of time to write, after I had kept the daily events and accounts in order – while they all cruised the world in a yacht.'

Penelope eyed him calmly.

'Weren't you lonely?'

'Very. That's why this is so wonderful.' She sensed a kind of euphoria – it shone from him. There was nothing to do but give in; the lobster was perfect, the champagne enhanced their discovery of one another; it was an evening, she knew, that happens once in a lifetime. It was past midnight when he left her at her door. He did not even wait to be thanked. Every corner of her champagne-tinted brain was a question mark. She went up the darkened stairs slowly, and let herself in to her darker flat; as she put on a lamp in her bedroom, she caught sight of her glowing self in the mirror.

'Curious,' she said aloud. She had dressed with so much care, and now as she took off chiffon nothings and put on her old warm bathrobe, her mind cleared a little. She asked herself what she had expected. His words did not match his behaviour, she decided. He had been silent as she fitted her key into the lock of her door, then he had turned like a dark shadow, and been swallowed up by the night. It wasn't fair. She was filled with a physical discontent. Too much champagne, she thought, and went into her kitchen and drank a glass of milk. The telephone rang. She knew it would be his voice; so she let it ring.

An hour later, just as she was going to sleep, it rang again. This time she answered.

'Yes?'

'Is that all?' His voice sounded muffled and strange. 'Why didn't you answer before?'

'I'm sorry. Is something the matter?'

'Not really. I left so quickly because I started this bloody asthma attack, but I had to say goodnight to you. Will I see you tomorrow please?' There was a pause. Then she said 'Of course', and they arranged to meet when she left the office at five o'clock.

When she put down the telephone, she sat on the edge of her bed in the dark. Waves of anxiety washed over her, and now added to this, compassion came creeping to destroy any self-discipline that might steady her. She had been taken so unawares. Finally, she slept and woke just in time to dress, gulp down a cup of coffee, and rush to her office. A memorandum lay in her desk asking her to see the Editor at once.

Miss Humbert, stout, sharp-nosed, with perfectly set hair and pearls in her ears, smiled her practised smile, and tapped her desk with a pencil held in her manicured fingers. She made Penelope feel untidy.

'Have you made up your mind about my suggestion yesterday? I must know this morning.'

'Actually I would like to take my holiday now.'

'That might be arranged, provided you come back ready to accept the new job.'

'I'm not sure I can do it.'

'Penelope: answer me – are you worried about something? Or involved in some emotional business that upsets you? I should have thought, the combination of travel and journalism was just your cup of tea. And of course you are perfect for the job.'

Penelope was tempted to tell the tycoonesss what troubled her; but even though they had been friends for six years, the knowledge of each other had not been deep or confiding. So she tightened her mind, and resolved the problem by refusing what was offered, knowing that by doing so, she might make a mild enemy or even lose an opportunity. But Miss Humbert surprised her:

'Go away and enjoy yourself, and come back fighting fit. I won't take "no" for an answer; and I'm sure you'll see the sense of what I say. Send me a postcard from wherever it is.' She got up and started pushing papers about on her desk. Penelope said 'Thanks,' and Miss Humbert smiled a chilly smile, as the glass door closed, leaving her alone, all-seeing and seen by all, in her waterless aquarium.

There was still the week to finish. Penelope went back to her desk feeling drunk with audacity, and not knowing what her next move would be. By the afternoon it had been decided for her. John invited her to go to Paris – and then on to the South to visit his friend Maurice Taylor and his wife, who had a villa near Vence. He said he had the tickets booked for Sunday.

'How dare you do that?'

'Because I knew you would come.'

She wasn't angry, just bewildered. And bewitched.

'How could you know I had asked for my holiday?'

'I didn't. I only thought if I invited you, you might ask the She-Dragon to let you have it. But you forestalled me.'

'You seem to know my mind better than I do!'

'That's as it should be. It makes it easier, because I'm not good at saying what I feel about you.'

'You don't know me enough to feel anything about me . . .'

He laughed: 'How stupid of you. I've known you all my life. Just never found you. Don't you realise that? Don't you feel anything about me?'

'Yes. Much more than I want to.'

'Good. Now let's see what time the plane leaves.'

He reached into the pocket of his shaggy tweed jacket and took out a shiny air-travel time table. They were sitting in a dull tea-shop near the office; over-brewed tea in thick white cups, and biscuits in cellophane, but to Penelope it might well have been the nectar-bar of the gods. They agreed not to see each other till they met at the airport on Sunday afternoon.

The next five days sped by. Penelope's imagination and expectation worked overtime. She bought some very simple, lovely clothes, and finished her weekly article for the magazine; tidied her desk, and walked about the office smiling at everyone, most of whom looked back in questioning glumness, as though no-one had any right to be happy. They all seemed to be doing penance for something.

Sunday dawned, bright, with spring clouds puffed in a pale sky, and of course she was far too early at the airport, and John far too late. The plane was being announced in hollow echoes through the tannoys as he arrived, breathless and beaming.

'Come on,' he said, seizing her hand, and almost running to the exit marked 'GATE 19'. She felt as if a pistol-shot had marked the start of a race. No time to think, just move, and somehow, get there.

John had telephoned from London to an old hotel on the Rue Jacob, St Germain. They were ushered into a room overlooking a courtyard. The wallpaper was a thicket of pink roses and emerald green leaves climbing a trellis, and a huge brass bed with a gold-coloured eiderdown folded like a croissant seemed to take up all available space. Madame flung open the shutters with aplomb, and the late afternoon sun spilled into the room like Midas-magic. The key with its black rubber ball and chain was handed over, and Madame trilled coyly,

'Monsieur's room is just down the hall – the key is in the door, number seventeen. I hope you will be comfortable.'

John said, 'I'll leave you to unpack. Knock at my door when you feel like it. The bathroom's at the end of the hall.' He closed the door softly and left Penelope standing by the window in the glow of the red sun, but feeling chilled to the bone.

How absurd women are, she thought. When she saw the big brass bed she had thought it was the answer. But John obviously side-stepped every romantic implication. And he must have been here before, she mused, because he knew where the bathroom was. She was in love with him, but she had the feeling that if she dared let him know it, a spell would be broken. Without seeing, without thinking, she walked up and down that cramped rose-ridden bedroom and told herself that it was the loving, not the being loved, that mattered. What nonsense. She would find out what was the matter, she would melt him down, all in good time. So she unpacked and chose a grey dress. Her gold chains would shine, and so would she. It was an hour before she was ready, and knocked at his door.

When John went to his room down the hall, he flung himself on the narrow bed and closed his eyes. He had never felt quite like this. There had been no involvements. Before he started writing he had had sessions with an analyst – who helped him over his adolescent misinterpretations. In his boyhood, his fanatical mother had tried to steer him to the priesthood – and when this failed she had told him over and over again that no woman could possibly enjoy sex, that it was ugly, and good women loathed it; that it bred misery and disgust. He soon realised her misguided theories were sad, mad and deplorable. All this did not help his asthmatic efforts to live normally as he grew up. Whenever he became excited he ended up in bed for three days, with a strange machine to assist his breathing: his half-mad mother would say gleefully that it was his punishment for evil thoughts. This, and her bitter arguments with his father, made him lose all respect for her. Fortunately a teacher at his school recognised his talent and his troubles, and sent him to the analyst. From then on, understanding himself at last, he worked hard and got his scholarship to Oxford. The only thing that remained were asthma attacks occasionally, and a mistrust of women. At Oxford he fell in love with his friend Maurice Taylor, who in turn was in love with a very intelligent and beautiful young woman, whom he married. She understood John – and listened and helped him. She had said: 'One day someone will come along and life will be simple and wonderful.' His modest success as a writer filled the next years – then came the job at the magazine and Penelope. And now there was a knock on the door.

'Come in – sorry, I haven't changed yet.'

Penelope appeared, looking sedate in her grey dress. She sat on his bed while he found a clean shirt, and chose a tie, as though she had always watched him as he dressed. They chatted comfortably about where they would go for dinner and what they would do the next day. As they left their keys with Madame at the desk, she smiled as only the French can, when they suspect intrigue, romance or mischief.

'She thinks we are lovers,' Penelope said as they walked out into the cool evening.

'Aren't we?'

She did not think that was funny, and told him so. He took her arm and said:

'I feel safe with you.'

'That's a dubious compliment.' John laughed. She felt raw on all her edges, but he seemed perfectly happy. They walked to an avenue where the chestnut trees were in bloom, and the petals showered down like confetti in the soft air. Side-walk cafés were full, their brightly lit interiors silhouetted the people enjoying their wines and coffees; the latin-rough voices cut the air, the laughter boomed and tinkled and filled the warm night. Couples walked, arms entwined and paused to kiss, whole families were strung out across the pavement, with sleepy children being dragged along on their bandied fat legs – a typical spring evening before the tourists invaded to change the rhythm of contentment.

It was all as it should be, Penelope told herself, knowing she wanted it to be quite different. They supped at a table the size of an onyx seal-ring, in a crowd sitting thigh to thigh, pungently aromatic, and mistaking each other's drinks, packed so close in their enjoyment. John was in a fine mood throughout the evening; at one moment he looked at her as though he had never seen her before, and said:

'I never realised you were beautiful.'

'It's the dress, perhaps?'

'No. It's the way you look at people. Your eyes drink them in, and start sparkling. Very exciting to watch.'

'Let's go,' she said.

They walked back to the hotel in silence. No-one was at the desk, so they took their keys and got into the two-foot square wrought-iron cage that vibrated them to the third floor. John opened her door. The moonlight was streaming into the room striking the brass bedstead into blazing stars – for a moment they stood there, moon-struck – and then John said, 'Come and say goodnight to me, before you sleep.'

She slipped past him into her room. Before she shut the door he said 'I must talk to you.'

Indeed he must. As she brushed her hair, she had questions and answers ready. She was too old, she reminded herself, to play games like some coy adolescent, and she felt mortally wounded, and tired. She remembered that he had promised nothing, asked for nothing, done nothing to nourish her senses. That he enchanted her was not his fault, he did not know what she felt. She wondered what he would do, if he knew. She would find out, this night – before they ventured further by a day. So, clothed in romantic truculence, and a most becoming dressing gown, she went along the sleeping corridor to Room 17.

He was sitting up in bed, reading; when she came in, he put down his book and held out his arms to her.

The night had not been a success. Towards dawn they started to talk in whispers, she sitting cross-legged at the foot of his bed, smoking.

'You see,' he said, 'I have never been physically involved with anyone. I suppose I fell in love with Maurice at Oxford, as I told you – but I never knew anything from him but kindness and rejection. I've never used the word "love". I've been afraid to. Somehow what I feel for you is beyond that. When I said I felt "safe" with you, that's what I meant.'

'But I'm in love with you. What shall I do?'

'Come with me to the South, if you can. Maurice and his wife are expecting us.'

'Have you any idea how awful that will be for me? How I will want to be close to you, and not dare to impose myself on you? Isn't it asking too much of me? Maybe your mad mother was right.'

'Right about what?'

'Your becoming a priest. John, listen to me: I'll try. Forget tonight. But I shall remember every inch of you. I could be quite happy with no rapture, no excitement, if I could be told that you finally knew what the word "love" could mean!'

She got up off his bed, smiled at him, and kissed him quickly on the forehead. She suffered the warm smell of his body; comfort and despair.

'Sleep now,' she whispered. 'We'll have a glorious day tomorrow – no – today. Let's go to the Île St Louis, and then eat at Café Paul in the Place Dauphine.'

She slipped out of his room. A valet was already in the hall, setting down polished shoes outside the door. He showed no surprise, but said a polite 'Bonjour Madame' as she opened her own door. Maybe all was right with the world.

It was midday when she woke up. A note was slipped under her door – it just said 'Café Paul, 1.30'. She dressed slowly, and felt strangely serene as she went out into the noon silence of the street, and hailed a taxi. John was waiting for her at one of the scrubbed pine tables in the famous Café Paul. It was crowded as usual, but with serious dignitaries of the law and church, who tumbled out of their splendid granite buildings nearby to eat and brood and talk for two hours. Again, there was a parcel at her place at table, this time a very small one tied with a gold and blue ribbon.

'Souvenir,' he said, 'and no knots to untie!'

She opened the little box. In it lay a silver egg, not much bigger than her thumbnail, etched over with a delicate tracery of leaves. It shone in the palm of her hand as though some bird had nested and left it pulsing there.

'It's beautiful! Thank you. I shall keep it always.'

'I hope so. The man in the antique shop said it was the smallest one ever made. Let's eat.'

They ordered lunch, and managed to talk of everyday things. When they had finished, the bill paid, the last drop of cognac sipped, Penelope told him she was not going South with him. She was not prepared for his reaction. The chair scraped harshly as he stood up, eyes blazing, and shook his head at her slowly, turned on his heel and was gone. Emptiness, grief and a marble numbness. When she got back to the hotel, he had already left, Madame said, leaving no message. She stayed in Paris two more days, believing she had done what was right for both of them.

Miss Humbert, the Editor, asked no questions when she returned so suddenly, and welcomed her to her new assignment. Months went by. She had no word from John and her mind adjusted to his silence and absence. She shone with success, but every time she opened her wardrobe door and saw the grey dress hanging there, unworn, accusing, a wave of questioning fury swept over her; even that subsided as she went on her efficient way and gave the dress to Oxfam.

One morning, two years later, she found a letter on her desk – a typewritten envelope with a South of France postmark. Her heart missed a beat and she left it unopened until all else had been attended to. But it was not from John. It came from his friend, Maurice Taylor. He felt she would want to know that John had decided to enter the priesthood and was in a monastery at Rheims. The letter said how sorry they had all been that she had not come to the South of France with John so long ago: 'things might have turned out differently'.

Penelope felt the old wounds opening. She closed her eyes. She had said to him that night: 'Maybe you should be a priest': but now she remembered the scrape of his chair as he got up to leave her in Café Paul, and the feel of her fingers closing around a little box. She must find it – it had suddenly become the most important thing in her world. When she got home from the office she searched everywhere. In the middle of the night, she sat up suddenly, remembering. Her feet bare, and in her nightdress, she brought her small step-ladder from the kitchen, and the lamplight not enough, she took her torch to find an old suitcase on a top-shelf – it still had a tag addressed to Paris tied to its handle. She opened it on her bed – inside was an umbrella, a paperback copy of Proust, a menu from Café Paul, and a very small box tied up with blue and gold ribbon. Her heart turned over. Inside the box the silver egg was shining – bright as a jewel. She turned and turned it. She had never suspected it would open, but here, almost hidden by the fine engraving, was a hair-line crack. Very gently she pulled the tiny egg apart. It was gold inside as though newly-minted. A tiny scrap of paper fell into the palm of her hand – on it, in John's neat, small writing, the words 'I *love* you'.